BEWARE!!
DO NOT READ THIS
BOOK FROM
BEGINNING TO END!

What a bummer! Your mom hired a clown to entertain at your birthday party. You're way too old for that kind of thing, you think. Until the "clown" shows up. And he's totally terrifying!

Dr. MacDeath has greenish skin, long, sharp fingernails, and pointy fangs that drip some kind of gooey red stuff all over your mom's carpet. Ugh! Before you can do anything, MacDeath nails shut all the doors in your house — and promises to give you the most horrifying birthday you've ever had!

This guy is so freaky, you've got a feeling he isn't kidding. Can you and your friends escape before MacDeath traps you in a world of unending horror?

This scary adventure is all about you. You decide what will happen. And you decide how terrifying the scares will be!

Start on *PAGE 1*. Then follow the instructions at the bottom of each page. You make the choices. If you choose well, you'll make it home again. But if you make the wrong choice . . . BEWARE!

SO TAKE A DEEP BREATH. CROSS YOUR FINGERS. AND TURN TO *PAGE 1* TO *GIVE YOURSELF GOOSEBUMPS*!

R.L. STINE

GIVE YOURSELF

Goosebumps®

SCARY BIRTHDAY
TO YOU!

AN
APPLE
PAPERBACK

SCHOLASTIC INC.
New York Toronto London Auckland Sydney
Mexico City New Delhi Hong Kong

A PARACHUTE PRESS BOOK

No part of this publication may be reproduced in whole or in part, or stored in a retrieval system, or transmitted in any form or by any means, electronic, mechanical, photocopying, recording, or otherwise, without written permission of the publisher. For information regarding permission, write to Scholastic Inc., Attention: Permissions Department, 555 Broadway, New York, NY 10012.

ISBN 0-590-99390-9

Copyright © 1999 by Parachute Press, Inc. All rights reserved. Published by Scholastic Inc. APPLE PAPERBACKS and logo are trademarks and/or registered trademarks of Scholastic Inc. GOOSEBUMPS is a registered trademark of Parachute Press, Inc.

12 11 10 9 8 7 6 5 4 3 2 1   9/9 0 1 2 3 4/0

Printed in the U.S.A.   40

First Scholastic printing, September 1999

Your best friend, Alex, walks into your living room on your birthday. He gazes around with a grin. "You're kidding! A birthday party — with no one home?"

"My parents had to work," you explain. "My older brother was supposed to hang out, but he split as soon as my parents left."

Your four other friends from school are already there. Josh. Mickey. Sarah. Virginia. Alex shoots a fist into the air. "Yes!"

He tosses a big, colorfully wrapped package at you. "Catch. It's your present. You're going to *love* it!" Alex says. "I talked my mom into spending double the limit — since it's you."

You grin and catch the gift on the fly. It feels like a whole bunch of video game cartridges wrapped up together. Awesome!

"Who else is invited?" Sarah asks.

"Gabe and Brittany," you answer. "But they both got sick. And the Boyter twins might not get home in time."

The doorbell rings, and Josh races to answer it.

"Par-ty! Par-ty!" Josh chants. He flings open the door.

You gasp at what's standing there.

Answer the door on PAGE 2.

2

You stare at the guy in the doorway. He's about six feet six inches tall — and hideous. His face is a grayish-green color, with big slash marks on it. His eyes are rimmed in red, and they're blood-shot. Long, greasy hair hangs down the sides of his head, but he's bald on top. His teeth are pointy, and they're dripping what looks like — blood.

It's makeup, you think. It's got to be.

But it looks amazingly real.

"Happy birthday," the guy says in a deep, booming voice. It sounds like pure evil. He stares straight at you.

"Who is that?" Alex whispers in your ear.

You shrug. Good question.

Then you notice all the stuff the guy is carrying. Three birthday presents. A big cake box from a nearby bakery. A black cloth bag filled with party favors. Could he be some kind of entertainer for your party? Like a clown or something?

He shoves his creepy face up close to yours. "I'm Dr. MacDeath," he says, lowering his voice to a hoarse whisper. "Your parents hired me for your party. You're into horror — right?"

"Horror? Uh, yeah." You gulp.

Let the freaky clown in on PAGE 3.

Dr. MacDeath pushes past you and marches into the living room.

Oh, brother, you think. How could your parents *do* this to you? Hire some guy to perform at your party? You're too old for clowns. And besides, this guy is seriously freaky.

You glance at your friends. They're really going to razz you for this.

Wait a minute — their faces are lighting up. Hey! They all seem to think this guy is cool. All except Sarah.

"Your parents hired a clown?" she asks in a snotty voice. "How babyish! What's he going to do — make balloon animals?"

"Sure," Dr. MacDeath says in his sinister voice. "But I forgot to bring balloons — so I'll have to use *you* instead!"

He grabs Sarah and lifts her up. With his long, strong arms, he begins pulling on her legs — twisting them!

"Owwwwww!" Sarah screams. "Let me go!"

"There!" Dr. MacDeath sets your friend on the floor. "What do you think?" He laughs a terrible, deep laugh.

Go on to PAGE 4.

You stare in horror at Sarah. What did MacDeath *do* to her?

Sarah doesn't look human anymore! MacDeath has stretched her arms and legs around her body so many times that now she looks like — a swan!

A balloon-animal swan!

"Help me," she moans.

You glance at your friends. Everyone looks about as horrified as you feel. But — this can't be real, right? It must be some kind of magic trick or something. If someone was really twisted up like that, they'd be a goner. Wouldn't they?

"Who's next?" MacDeath demands. He points at Josh. "You?"

"Nooo!" Josh cries. His voice cracks as he backs away.

"Stop it!" Alex shouts at MacDeath. "And put Sarah back to normal!"

Dr. MacDeath eyes Sarah. "Normal?" he says. "She looks pretty normal to me!" He lets loose another crazy laugh.

Oh, no, you think. This guy is a lunatic! You don't know whether to scream or run to get your older brother, Brian.

But before you can decide, the front doorbell rings.

"Don't answer it!" Dr. MacDeath shouts.

Should you listen to him?

If you answer the front door, turn to PAGE 41.
If you don't answer it, turn to PAGE 60.

The head in the bakery box stares up at you.

And then — whoa!

Its dead-looking yellow eyes blink, its lips move.

"Help me," the head pleads, moving its mouth with great effort. "Please . . . help me."

You want to barf. Or at least push the box off your lap.

Your stomach turns over. You feel faint . . . and sick . . . and terrified. All at once.

Get this thing off me! you think.

But something stops you. Stops you from jumping up. Shoving the box away.

It's the look in the head's eyes — so real.

And so sad.

"Help me — please," he pleads again, sounding desperate.

Help him on PAGE 97.

"Wow!" Josh says with a shiver. "That was . . . way too weird!"

"Yeah," Alex agrees. "I guess your parents did hire him for your party after all."

You slowly nod your head. "I guess so."

"But what did he mean about 'see you tomorrow'?" Sarah asks.

You shrug. Who knows?

Then it hits you.

"Wait a second. Tomorrow's the first day of school!" you remind your friends.

Yup. That's right.

When you arrive at school the next day, a tall man with a deep voice is standing out front. His face isn't green anymore. And his teeth don't drip blood. But it's the same guy. You can tell from the twisted sneer on his face.

"Good morning," he says. He grins at you. "I'm Dr. MacDermott — your new school principal. If you don't follow the rules — you're going to be *very* sorry!"

He laughs the same evil laugh that you heard yesterday.

You and Alex glance at each other.

You can't believe it. Your new principal is a real horror — and the school year looks like it's going to be a total nightmare!

THE END

"Let's leave Virginia here," Josh suggests. "She's such a wimp anyway. She won't be any good at finding stuff on the list."

"No way!" Virginia objects. "I'm not staying here with him! It's *your* birthday." She points at you. "*You* should stay."

"Yeah," Sarah chimes in. "He's *your* party guy. You stay with him!"

She's right, you think. You probably *should* be the one to stay behind.

But then maybe your friends will just go home. Maybe they'll *never* come back for you. Maybe you'll be stuck with Dr. MacDeath — forever!

Well?

If you leave Virginia with Dr. MacDeath, turn to PAGE 44.

If you stay with Dr. MacDeath yourself, turn to PAGE 106.

You feel your throat tighten up, staring at the photo of yourself on the CD.

"Alex? What is this — some kind of a sick joke?" you ask.

"I don't know anything about it," Alex blurts out fast. "Honest! I bought you a bunch of music CDs." Alex points at MacDeath. "He must have changed it — somehow!"

"Play it!" Dr. MacDeath orders in his hoarse voice.

You can't, you realize. You're frozen to your spot.

MacDeath grabs the CD from your hands and quickly puts it in the player in your living room.

Organ music booms out of the speakers. Creepy organ music. Like from an old horror film.

Then you hear your own voice in the background.

Your own voice — begging and pleading for help!

"No!" you hear yourself scream on the CD. "Don't hurt me! Leave me alone!"

Listen to the rest on PAGE 63.

Dr. MacDeath drags Mickey into the dark house. You, Alex, and the others follow.

Where did Mickey get a murderer's knife, anyway? you wonder.

And what's Dr. MacDeath going to do with it?

Sarah rushes ahead of you, to find Virginia. Virginia is huddled on a big chair, hugging her knees.

"Did he hurt you?" Sarah asks.

"No," Virginia whimpers. "But he made me watch while he ate live bugs. It was horrible!"

"Ewww!" Sarah cries, making a face.

"And he said he's never going to let us go!" Virginia adds.

"Shut up!" MacDeath shouts. "All of you — just shut up!"

Wait a minute — why should we? you wonder.

Maybe you should start screaming. Make tons of noise, so the neighbors will call the police.

"Let's see what you've brought me, you little scavengers," MacDeath says with a chuckle. "Let's see if you won the game."

What do you think? Do you want to start screaming? Or see if you won the scavenger hunt?

If you start screaming, turn to PAGE 37.

If you shut up and hope you've won the game, turn to PAGE 21.

You open the back door for Mrs. Jancovich.

"Who threw this into my garden?" she demands. She hands you the bomb.

Now that you're not in panic mode, you can see that the "bomb" is made of cheap plastic. It's just a toy.

You talk fast. "This guy was trying to kill us." You point to MacDeath. "He — he twisted Sarah into a swan!"

"Uh, actually — no, he didn't," Sarah calls from behind you.

"What?" You whirl around to face her.

"This is my uncle Ted," Sarah explains. "The whole thing was supposed to be a surprise. To make your party scary. See, I'm double-jointed. Uncle Ted taught me how to twist my arms and legs like that, into a swan." She chuckles. "Pretty freaky, huh?"

"Your mother told me about this party." Mrs. Jancovich scowls. "It's obviously gotten out of hand. Which means it's over — right now. Send all your friends home."

What a bummer! I can't believe it, you think, as your friends file out the door. This whole scary birthday was a trick! A show put on by Sarah and her uncle Ted!

Well, believe it or not, that's the truth.

And you'll have to decide whether to believe us when we tell you you've reached

THE VERY BEST END IN THE WHOLE BOOK.

Okay, you think. Alex is right. You'll hang the doll from the end of the branch.

You creep out on the tree limb and try to balance there, fiddling with the noose.

Then you slip it around the doll's neck and let her fall.

She swings there for a minute, hanging by her neck.

A shiver runs up your spine.

This is totally sick, you think. You tremble, clinging to the tree branch.

The branch begins to quiver and shake.

Whoa! You're starting to slip. All of a sudden, you can't *wait* to come down from that tree!

Come on down on PAGE 62.

The floor shakes and rumbles so much that you and your friends all stop screaming, to see what's going on.

"Whoa!" Josh cries. "Earthquake!"

He's right. You see some glasses shake and jiggle on a shelf.

A moment later, you notice a siren. A number of sirens. Really loud, piercing ones.

"What *is* that?" Virginia asks meekly. "Are the police coming? To save us?"

You listen for a minute.

Nope. That's only car alarms! Car alarms set off by a small earthquake — which is now over.

"Ha-ha-ha!" Dr. MacDeath laughs. "You little fools! No one heard your stupid screams — and now, because of my beautiful earthquake, no one will! Those car alarms are going to be blaring for the next two hours!"

Your heart sinks. MacDeath's magic caused that earthquake. He's so powerful. How are you ever going to get out of this?

"Now," MacDeath insists, "show me what you found on the scavenger hunt. That's the only way you're going to get out of here alive."

Do what he says on PAGE 21.

Bob points to a coffin in the middle of a small, dungeon-like room.

You stop short.

In the coffin you see the body of a boy, in Josh's clothes. It's laid out like a corpse — and it has no head!

"Aaaaah!" you scream.

Did they really cut off Josh's head?

"Great scream!" Bob says cheerfully, holding a small, handheld tape recorder in front of your face. "I *knew* you'd be good at this!"

"But, but . . ." you stammer.

Bob laughs and walks over to the corpse. "Don't worry — it's not real," he explains. "We just borrowed your friend's clothes, to give you a good scare."

He slaps the rubber corpse to show you.

"But wait till you see what we did with your pet cat!" he adds with a nasty smile.

Well — go on. Scream again. You're getting paid for it! So you might as well scream your head off, all the way to . . .

THE END.

14

Sweating with fear, you stare at the bomb you've just caught.

It's going to explode! you think. It'll blow me to bits!

You turn and hurl it as hard and as fast as you can. You throw it straight through the nearest window, shattering the glass.

It lands outside — in a flower bed in your next-door neighbor's yard.

"Take cover, everyone!" you shout. "Duck!"

Turn to PAGE 39.

You point your weapon at Dr. MacDeath and pull the trigger.

KA-BLAM! A green paintball flies out of the barrel. It smacks him hard — right in the middle of his chest.

"Good shot!" Dr. MacDeath cheers.

Then instantly he fires his weapon at you.

SPLAT!

You're been blasted with a ton of the liquid acid.

You're history! Toast.

The stuff in MacDeath's weapon has eaten you for dinner.

BURP!

THE END

"Let's go drown him in paintballs," you decide.

Huddled in the bushes, you and your friends all load up your weapons.

Then you take a deep breath.

Where is MacDeath, anyway?

Outside the bushes, it's quiet.

You hear a twig snap. Was that a footstep? Nearby?

Your heart pounds, as you wonder. Is MacDeath waiting out there? Waiting to ambush you?

What if he blasts you first — with that acid stuff? Right in the face?

"On my signal," you whisper to Alex, "we go!"

Alex nods.

"Now!" you say as softly as you can.

Leap out of the bushes on PAGE 53.

"Let's play Pin the Tail on the Donkey," you decide.

It's a stupid game, you realize. Really babyish. But you picked it because if *babies* can play it, then you figure it'll be pretty safe. No one will get hurt doing it. Will they?

Besides, you have a plan. You're going to cheat — and peek. It's worth it if you can beat Dr. MacDeath.

"Yes." Dr. MacDeath gives an evil grin. "Pin the Tail. Gooood."

He reaches into his black bag and pulls out a large cardboard cutout of an animal. It looks more like a huge, ugly dog than a donkey. Its face is turned toward you, and it seems to be growling. It has very sharp teeth.

Dr. MacDeath tapes the thing right onto your living room wall.

"What *is* that thing?" Alex asks.

Dr. MacDeath doesn't answer. He just snickers to himself.

You shiver at the sneaky look on his face. What could MacDeath have up his sleeve?

The game begins on PAGE 115. Get ready to win — or lose!

18

Your heart is pounding as you glance at the four items on the table.

"Uh, I'll pick the drain cleaner," you decide.

Why not? you think. The others don't seem right. The mouse's tongue is *inside* a whole mouse. Maybe MacDeath won't like that. The noose wasn't used to hang a real person. And the skeleton? For all you know, it's plastic!

"The drain cleaner?" MacDeath shouts. "You call *that* a *pretty* poison? Ha-ha-ha! What a joke! You lose!"

Then he whips a pack of matches and some birthday candles out of his pocket. He jabs a handful of candles into your birthday cake. The cake full of bugs.

"Time to make a wish!" he yells, gleefully lighting the candles. "And I'll give you a hint. Before I'm done with you — you'll wish you were dead!"

The candles are grouped so close together, they all flame up at once. Like a huge torch. The flames singe the ceiling. Gobs of wax drip onto the cake.

"Whoa!" Alex shouts. "Blow them out — before he burns the house down!"

Blow out the candles on PAGE 25.

"I am not touching a dead mouse," you insist as you hurry toward the pet store.

It's a long walk — about ten blocks away — to the store. It takes you twenty minutes to get there. When you arrive, the shop owner is just closing up.

"Please," you beg him. "We just need to buy a mouse."

"Okay," the shop owner says. "I've got one right here — real cheap. But be quick about it."

Hastily the owner lifts a small gray mouse out of a cage. He puts it in a cardboard container — the kind that Chinese food comes in. You pay the man and leave.

Then you race back to your neighborhood.

But by the time you get there, the hour is almost up.

"We've got to meet the others back at my house in eight minutes!" you exclaim. "And we don't have the noose. Or the blood from a turnip!"

"We're going to lose," Alex moans. "We blew it. We're dead!"

Hurry to PAGE 57.

"Hey, Dr. MacDeath," you call. "Uh, how many birthday parties do you do a week?"

MacDeath eyes you sideways.

"Why do you want to know?" he asks.

"Because," you mumble. "I was thinking ... maybe you need an assistant."

"An assistant?" MacDeath repeats. He seems to turn the idea over in his head.

"Yeah," you explain. "You know — someone to help you out at the parties. Carry your black bag. Help you scare kids. Stuff like that."

Please say yes, you think. Let me be your assistant.

Because as soon as Dr. MacDeath lets you leave the house, you can call the police! Or run for help. Get away from him somehow.

MacDeath's face lights up. "Yeah," he agrees. "Maybe I do need a sidekick!"

Yes! you think. He went for it!

Become MacDeath's assistant on PAGE 40.

You decide to do what MacDeath says. Shut up and show him the stuff you've found.

He marches over to the dining room table and pats it.

"Here," he says. "Put all the little goodies right here."

One by one, you lay your three things on the table. The mouse, the turnip, and the noose. Josh adds the skeleton's hand and the drain cleaner — the "pretty" poison. Mickey goes last. He reaches into his pocket and pulls out a Swiss army knife.

"Ah-ha!" Dr. MacDeath cries.

He snatches up the knife and quickly sticks it under his nose. He sniffs. Deeply. Twice.

"Yesss," he says. "This *is* a murder weapon! I can smell the lovely stench of death on the blade!"

You shiver and stare at Mickey in alarm. Is it *really*? A real *murderer's knife*? Where did he get it?

And can Dr. MacDeath *really* smell death on the blade?

Sick!

"Well, well, well," MacDeath says. "Perhaps you *are* going to win this game."

See if you've won on PAGE 90.

"I want to . . . um . . . open presents." You try to control your trembling voice.

"Good," Dr. MacDeath says, staring at you with his hideous, red-rimmed eyes.

He grins and reaches for the three wrapped presents he brought with him. One tiny box. A medium-size package. And a large one wrapped in shiny black paper with ugly green ribbons.

"Want to open my presents," he asks, "or those wimpy gifts from your so-called *friends*?"

An evil smile forms at the corners of his mouth.

He looks like he can't wait for you to choose. Because either way, it's going to be horrible!

You swallow hard.

The way he looks, you feel scared to open *anything*!

But you've got to pick something.

If you open Dr. MacDeath's gifts, turn to PAGE 75.

If you open gifts from your friends, turn to PAGE 100.

Dr. MacDeath lets the other kids at your party go home. Then he drives you and Josh to Horror Place.

When you reach the amusement park, Dr. MacDeath hops out of the car and watches you go through Horror Place's big black wrought-iron gates.

They're twisted into the shape of a huge skull.

"Bye," he calls. For some reason his voice sounds as if he's mocking you. "Have tons of fun — *my* kind of fun!"

"Good-bye — and good riddance!" Josh calls back in a snotty tone of voice.

"Hey, don't make him mad," you caution Josh. "We don't want him coming after us or anything."

"Don't worry about it. We're home free now!" Josh says. "Last one in the haunted house is a rotten egg!" He races ahead of you into the huge, creepy house that is the central attraction at Horror Place. It's painted black, with bright green slime dripping all over it.

"Wait!" you call to Josh, running to catch up with him.

You dash in through the double doors — and plunge into darkness. "Josh?" you call out softly in the dark.

But there's no answer.

Search for Josh on PAGE 68.

24

You make your choice.

"Dodgeball? Good!" Dr. MacDeath says. "All right, you know the rules. Make a circle — around me."

"Right here? In the living room?" you ask. "My mom always makes us play dodgeball outside!"

That's why you picked this game in the first place! You figured if you were outside, at least you could run for help.

But Dr. MacDeath shakes his head.

"In here!" he yells. "A circle! Now!"

You hear a clap of thunder outside. The sky darkens. You gulp. It's as if MacDeath's anger *caused* the thunder.

Your heart pounds in your ears. Oh, man. Who — or *what* — is this guy?

You, Alex, Sarah, Virginia, Josh, and Mickey all form a circle around Dr. MacDeath.

"Where's the ball?" Josh asks in a meek voice.

"Right here," MacDeath snarls. He bends over and reaches into his big black cloth bag.

But what he pulls out isn't a ball.

"No!" Mickey cries when he sees the object in the palm of MacDeath's hand. "Noooo!"

Dodge whatever it is on PAGE 112.

You take a deep breath and lean in close to the cake.

Make a wish? you think. That's easy. There's only one thing you *really* want.

You close your eyes and blow as hard as you can. . . .

I wish I was as far away from Dr. MacDeath as possible, you think.

You open up your eyes again.

Surprise! It's your birthday . . . so of course you got your wish!

You gaze around and see you've been transported to some kind of a small, undeveloped village. Straw huts stand all around you. You're in the middle of a dusty street — surrounded by what look like — llamas!

Yikes! Talk about scary!

But, hey — don't worry. If you can tough it out in this village for a year, maybe someone will make you another birthday cake. You'll get another wish, and you can try wishing yourself back home!

THE END

You heart hammers as you enter the ballroom.

"Josh?" you call, staring hard at the ghostly figures that are waltzing around the ballroom, faster and faster, in time to the music.

A chill runs up your spine.

It's just the creepy music that's making me scared, you tell yourself. If they'd turn off the music, it wouldn't be half so creepy in there.

Yeah, right. Then how come you just flinched when a wispy cobweb trailed across your face?

"Josh?"

"Yeah?" His voice comes from somewhere in the room. He sounds scared.

You squint harder, trying to see. . . .

Is that him? Dancing with the old woman with the long white hair?

"Help me," Josh calls. "She won't let me go!"

Help him on PAGE 111.

Alex pulls a thick rope out of a kitchen drawer and starts twisting it into a noose.

"Stephanie — my little sister Laura's doll," he answers, breaking into a goofy grin. "Laura thinks she's real, so we'll make a noose and hang her. That way, we can tell MacDeath that the noose was used to hang someone."

Whew! you think. Alex is talking about a doll. Well, hanging a little girl's doll is pretty cruel. But a regular old rope may not make it with Dr. MacDeath.

This is the best you can do.

Alex marches off toward his little sister's room and returns a moment later with the doll.

"Now we find a tree branch," Alex says.

"Okay," you agree. "Let's go."

Hang Stephanie on PAGE 55.

You stare at Josh's back — where MacDeath shot him. He's covered in — in paint!

You breathe a sign of relief. Whew! MacDeath was just firing a paintball gun.

"Owww!" Josh screams. "Helllp! Ow!"

What's his problem? It's just a paintball.

Then you notice the smoke rising from Josh's back. The paint! It looks as if it's burning Josh's clothes!

You grab the garden hose and turn the spray on Josh. Whatever is in Dr. MacDeath's paintball gun — it isn't paint! It's more like acid!

Washing the stuff off seems to help. But Josh's back looks horrible. Red and yucky — like it's going to blister.

"Ha-ha-ha!" Dr. MacDeath laughs. "Now . . . who's next?"

No way, you think. It's not going to be me — or any of us!

You raise your weapon to shoot back at him.

"Go ahead," he says. He stands at the far opposite end of the driveway, aiming his weapon filled with acid stuff at you. "Take your best shot," he challenges, smiling.

Uh-oh. Your heart pounds.

Are you fast enough for this showdown?

If you go for the showdown, turn to PAGE 15.
If you run and hide in the bushes, turn to PAGE 118.

Of course she's going to make fun of you.

Sarah's a really great friend. But she *hates* anything babyish.

"What a ridiculous party! I can't believe your parents hired a clown. What are you, *five*?" she asks you. "Come on, everybody, let's go." She heads for the door.

"Wait!" you cry, turning to your other friends. "You guys want to watch me open presents, don't you? That would be fun."

"No, thanks," Josh says. "I'm going home. I've had enough *fun* for one day."

"Me too," the other kids say.

Whoa! Talk about a lousy birthday!

When all your friends are gone, you light your birthday candles and make a wish. "I wish my birthday could start all over again," you say out loud.

Hey — no problem. To make your wish come true all you have to do is turn back to *PAGE 1* and start reading again!

But you *can't* wish your way out of the fact that you've come to . . .

THE END.

Alex backs away from you — as if you're a monster.

"No! I'm not going to cut the tongue out!" you explain quickly. "All we have to do is bring back a *whole* mouse — with the tongue inside. I mean, the list doesn't say the tongue has to be *detached* or anything."

"True," Alex agrees with a sigh of relief. Then his eyes light up. "Hey — I know where we can get a mouse!"

"Where?" you ask.

"My basement. My dad put a mousetrap down there a few days ago," Alex explains. "My mom complained because he didn't take away the dead mouse. Maybe it's still there."

A dead mouse? Yuck! "I was thinking we could go to the pet store and buy a live mouse," you suggest.

"That might take too long," Alex argues. "We've got to hurry. We still need two other things — the noose and the blood from the turnip. Which both sound pretty hard to come by."

He's right. The clock is ticking on you.

It's your birthday — so it's your call.

Mouse tongue: dead or alive?

If you go to Alex's basement for the dead mouse, turn to PAGE 54.

If you go to the pet store, turn to PAGE 19.

31

You blink again. And gasp.

Towering over you is . . .

A guy in khakis and a navy blue polo shirt?

Yes. A normal, regular guy. No scary makeup. No fangs dripping blood. Just a nice-looking college student with bushy eyebrows and a big smile.

"Hey — great scream," he says. He reaches out to offer you a hand. "I'm Bob Morton. I'm in charge of sound effects here at Horror Place. You want a job as a screamer?"

"A screamer?" you ask, bewildered.

"Yeah — doing sound effects," Bob explains. "We've got a ton of spooky rooms in this place. We use screaming sounds in most of them — on tape. But you're better than the stuff we've got. So I want to hire you and retape the screams. I'll pay you tons of money. What do you say?"

For tons of money you say yes — as fast as you possibly can!

"But what about my friend Josh?" you ask. "He disappeared in here a few minutes ago."

"Oh, don't worry," Bob says, leading you into one of the smaller rooms. "We gave him a job too. He's right here."

See what Josh is doing on PAGE 13.

A terrible, twisted smile creeps across Dr. MacDeath's face.

"The condition," he says, leering at you and your friends, "is that one of you must stay behind, here with me!"

"No way!" Josh argues. "That's kidnapping!"

MacDeath folds his arms over his chest and glares at you.

"If you want to have the scavenger hunt, one of you must stay behind as my prisoner!" he demands. "That way I'll be sure the rest of you will return."

You gulp and swallow hard. But you know this is your only chance. You've got to go along with it. And leave someone behind.

But who?

Decide on PAGE 7.

You open Mickey's pocketknife and cut the vegetable in half. Red juice runs onto the tablecloth, staining it a deep blood color. "See? Blood from a turnip!" you announce.

Dr. MacDeath throws back his greasy head and laughs. "You fool!" he shouts. "You're *beaten*. Because that's not a turnip — it's a beet! Ha-ha-ha-ha-ha!"

Oh, no, you think. It's not a turnip!

Your heart feels like it's pounding a thousand times a minute.

You can't believe it. You lost!

Turn to PAGE 114.

The acid in Dr. MacDeath's own weapon hits him. He grabs his face.

"Aaahhhhhh!" he cries, twisting in pain.

Then he pulls his hands away from his face. And grins.

A terrible, evil, vicious grin.

"You thought you could hurt me?" he asks. He tosses his head back and laughs.

You're definitely not finding this as funny as MacDeath.

You stare at him in horror as his face begins to twist . . . and grow. It puffs up — as if it's going to explode!

"What's going on?" Alex cries, gasping.

Your heart is pounding so hard, you can't answer him.

All you can do is watch . . . as Dr. MacDeath's head grows larger. And larger.

His body starts to expand too. As if the stuff you squirted at him was some kind of . . . madman fertilizer!

"Oh, no!" Virginia screams. "He's getting bigger!"

Turn to PAGE 103.

You and Alex exchange terrified glances. Where did this guy get the key to *your* back door?

"Now," Dr. MacDeath says. He picks up the big bakery box and sets it down on the dining room table. "Who wants cake?"

None of your friends move.

MacDeath reaches into his black cloth bag and pulls out a huge knife. "Here." He hands the knife to you. "You're the birthday kid. Cut the cake."

You take the long, gleaming knife from Dr. MacDeath. It's heavy and sharp — and deadly looking. You really don't want to hold it, but MacDeath thrusts the handle at you.

"Don't cut the cake until he fixes Sarah," Virginia demands. "Make him put her back to normal!"

"Oh, please," Dr. MacDeath says. He rolls his ugly, red-rimmed eyes. "Just cut the cake!"

"No!" you insist. "Not until you fix Sarah!"

MacDeath glares at you angrily.

What's he going to do? Turn to PAGE 104 to find out.

You lift the heavy bakery box off your lap and set it on the floor.

"Okay," you agree reluctantly. "Wait here. I'll go dig up your body."

"Wait here?" the head moans. "What is that — a joke? I *have* to wait here, wise guy! What choice do I have?"

He's got a point.

You grab a shovel and dash outside to Mrs. Jancovich's house.

"Are you nuts?" Alex asks, following you. "You're really going to dig up her flower garden? She'll kill you!"

"*They'll* kill us," you reply, nodding back toward the house where Dr. MacDeath and the severed head are. "Unless we help."

Alex shrugs and pitches in to do some digging. You both take turns digging up the flower garden. Under the moonlight.

Finally you come to it. The body. The headless dead body that was attached to the man in the bakery box.

Except it isn't really dead!

Turn to PAGE 122.

You start screaming at the top of your lungs.

"Hellllp! Aaaahhhhhhh!"

"Stop it!" MacDeath cries.

"NO!" you shout. "Come on, everybody! Scream your brains out! And maybe someone will come to help!"

Instantly, all your friends open their mouths and start screaming too.

You notice the dining room table beginning to shake.

Wow! you think. They're screaming so loud, it's making the floor rumble!

Turn to PAGE 12.

"Hey — cool!" you cheer. You stare into the box.

Inside is a gray stuffed animal about the size of a small dog. But it's a wolf. A gray wolf, with white fangs and pale blue eyes.

You reach into the box to feel the soft, fake fur.

"What is it?" Josh asks. He cranes his neck to see.

"It's a wolf!" you tell him. You put your hand on the stuffed animal's neck.

"Grrrrr . . ."

From inside the box, you hear a horrible growl. You stare at the wolf — and see what looks like — a flash in its eyes!

No, you think. It can't be. The stuffed animal can't be coming to life!

As fast as you can, you jerk your hand out of the box.

But not fast enough.

With one furious flick of his jaw, the wolf snaps at your hand and . . .

Whoops!

Looks like it'll be a little hard to turn the pages of this book from now on! Because you have come to a very *unhandy* . . .

END.

You and your friends lie on the floor and wait. You hold your breath, bracing yourself. Waiting for the deadly bomb explosion.

Nothing happens for an entire minute.

Then you hear your neighbor Mrs. Jancovich come out of her house.

"Uh-oh," MacDeath says in a whiny voice. His shoulders slump. "I'm in big trouble now."

Huh? Is Dr. MacDeath — this crazy, scary person — afraid of Mrs. Jancovich?

Find out on PAGE 71.

"So where's our next party?" you ask him. "We ought to get going, don't you think?"

"Yeah, sure," Dr. MacDeath agrees. "I've got another party across town in two hours. Maybe we should show up early — and scare the stupid birthday kid out of his mind! Ha-ha-ha-ha!"

You shiver when you hear him laugh. But you nod your head.

"Yeah," you agree. "Let's go early. That'll be good."

You and Dr. MacDeath climb into his car. It's a long black hearse — the kind of car used to drive dead people to the cemetery.

MacDeath drives across town and parks in front of a large brick house.

Now is my chance, you think. I'll bolt out of the car and make a dash for it. Run to freedom.

But something stops you.

Find out what it is on PAGE 82.

DINGDONG. DINGDONG. DINGDONG.

The doorbell rings three more times. As though it's really urgent that whoever's on the outside gets in.

You can't stand it. You have to answer the door. You run to it before Dr. MacDeath can stop you.

Please, you pray. Please let it be someone who can help us!

Maybe it's your friends the Boyter twins. Maybe their parents will be with them! Maybe they'll save you from this maniac!

Nope.

Standing in the doorway is a clown in full makeup. A party clown. White face. Red wig. Stupid polka-dot pants.

And he's holding a huge, sharpened hatchet in his hands!

Yikes!

Turn to PAGE 59.

"Aaaaahhhhh!" you scream. You jump back to get away from the bony hand.

But as you whirl around, you see Josh standing there. Mickey and Sarah are beside him. They burst out laughing.

"Gotcha!" Josh says. He shakes a skeleton's hand in your face.

"Very funny," you snap, not thinking it was funny at all. Isn't anyone else worried about Virginia? you wonder.

"Did you guys get everything?" Josh asks.

You nod. "How about you?"

"Sort of," Sarah says. "My dad had that skeleton's hand at home. We're using that for the bones."

"And I found some drain cleaner under our kitchen sink," Josh offers. "For the poison. It's not *pretty* poison, but it's the best I could do."

Oh, man, you think. That's pretty lame. "What about the murderer's knife?" you ask.

"I have one," Mickey answers solemnly. "You want to see it?"

"*I* want to see it!" a deep voice booms from inside the house. Dr. MacDeath flings open the back door. He grabs Mickey by the arm. "Give me the murderer's knife — now!"

Give him the knife on PAGE 9.

You swallow hard. But you decide Alex is right. If you're going to win the scavenger hunt, you've got to bring Dr. MacDeath *human* bones. That's what he meant when he said "bones from a grave-yard."

You grip the shovel and tiptoe toward the tomb-stones.

"Noooooooo," the spooky voice calls again.

But you ignore it. You stick your shovel into the ground and dig up a huge chunk of fresh earth.

WHOOSH! A forceful wind blows your hair back.

A white mist rises up out of the ground.

It looks like a long, almost human-shaped stream of smoke.

"I said noooooooo!" the spirit moans, swirling around your head.

Before you can run, the spirit twists its body around your neck — like a rope. Then it swirls again, twisting around Alex's neck. It has you both trapped!

"Only the dead walk here at night!" the spirit moans. It dives back into the freshly dug earth — dragging you with it!

Well, it looks like you've dug your own grave this time!

THE END

44

You tilt your head at Virginia. "Sorry," you tell her softly. "But we *have* to win — or we'll never get rid of that creep. Josh is right — you're not really good at scavenger hunts. So you stay here. We'll come back soon. I promise."

"No fair!" Virginia cries. Her eyes are wild with terror.

"Relax," Dr. MacDeath says to her. "We'll just hang around — and eat birthday cake together! Ha-ha-ha-ha-ha!"

He slices off a piece of cake. Two lizards scamper out from it. They run onto the table and then dart across the floor.

Virginia screams.

You feel bad, but you have no choice. You have to leave Virginia behind. You swallow hard and pick up the list of items. Then you turn to Dr. MacDeath.

"Unlock the back door," you demand. "Let us out."

You'll be free as soon as he unlocks the door on PAGE 83.

You glance to the corner of the room where the presents are stacked. A big box from Sarah sits near the front.

"Sarah?" you ask, eyeing her questioningly. "Should I open yours?"

You're a little nervous after what happened with Alex's present. But Sarah nods.

"Yeah — I guess so," she says.

You lift the big box and set it in the middle of the floor. It's wrapped in pink-and-purple paper, with HAPPY BIRTHDAY written all over it in silver ink.

"Hurry up!" Dr. MacDeath's scratchy voice booms at you.

Okay, here goes, you think.

You tear the wrapping off and open the big white gift box.

See what's inside on PAGE 38.

Are you serious?

You're going to tell Dr. MacDeath that his game isn't *fair*?

You want *fair* — from a madman? From a guy who twisted one of your best friends into a swan?

Forget it. Don't even go there.

Just close this book and come back when you're ready to face the facts.

Like the fact that no one named Dr. *MacDeath* gives a flying leap about playing fair.

And like the fact that — whether it's fair or not — you're being kicked out of this book for being too silly to read it!

THE END

You're about to say "Let's do it," when Mickey grabs your arm.

"Wait. *I* have a better idea," he announces. "I say we trick him into putting down his weapon. Then we take his weapon — and switch it with one of ours. If we have his gun, we can shoot him with that acid stuff."

Hmmm. That's a good plan too!

Well? What do you think you should do?

If you drown MacDeath in paintballs, turn to PAGE 16.

If you try to switch weapons with MacDeath, turn to PAGE 124.

"Your parents hired me for your party," the clown explains. "But that creep — MacDeath — kidnapped me and locked me in his basement. Then he started dropping in on birthday parties — *my* parties — all over town. Seems he gets a kick out of scaring kids to death. Now we've finally caught him."

"Wow," Alex says, shaking his head.

"But what about Sarah?" you ask. "Can you undo *that*?"

You turn and point at her — the human swan. You shudder.

"Don't worry — I can fix it," the clown answers you. "Balloon animals are my specialty. So I'll just . . . *un*make her!"

He picks up Sarah and tucks her under one arm. Then he begins twisting her arms and legs. *Untwisting* them, actually. Pretty soon she's back to normal.

Except that her face is all red. Her arms look sore. And she looks mad.

Sarah narrows her eyes at you.

"Your parents *did* hire a clown!" she complains. "How lame!"

Huh? Is she really going to make fun of you — even after you practically saved her life?

Find out on PAGE 29.

"Hold on!" you cry. "We still win!"

"How?" MacDeath asks, eyeing you carefully.

"Well, you didn't say the bones had to be *buried*," you argue. "You just said they had to be bones from a graveyard. And these were in a graveyard tonight. Weren't they, Sarah?"

You sort of give her a strong, steady stare. Like a hint — to tell MacDeath what you need him to hear.

"Uh, yeah, they were," Sarah says. She nods quickly. "We carried them into the graveyard on our way here."

MacDeath's shoulders slump. He stuffs the hammer and spike back into his bag. "Fine," he agrees glumly. "You win."

Whoa! Is that it? you think. Is MacDeath letting you go? Was he really just a party entertainer after all? But what about that lightning, and the buggy birthday cake, and his big, blood-dripping teeth?

He glances at his watch.

"Oops! I'm running late for my next party! I tell you, I'll be so glad when this summer job is over," he says.

He marches to the front door and pulls out the spike.

"Well, happy birthday!" he calls as he steps out the front door. "See you tomorrow!"

Tomorrow? What's *that* supposed to mean?

Find out on PAGE 6.

"Helllppp!" you scream.

The rat darts across the damp basement floor. Toward your feet! It's going to bite me, you think, choking with fear.

The flashlight that Alex is holding — the only light in the room — blinks out!

You're standing in complete darkness — with a rat racing toward your feet!

"Ahhhhh!" you scream. You rise up on your tiptoes, trying to get as far off the floor as you can. You hop from one foot to the other. You won't let that rat get you!

Alex fumbles with the flashlight, tapping it. Finally it blinks back on.

"Where'd the rat go?" you gasp, glancing in every direction at once.

"I don't know," Alex replies. "Let's just get the mouse and get out of here."

Pick up the mouse on PAGE 91.

"I'll take the little box," you announce to Dr. MacDeath.

Why not? you think. It's so small, how bad can the present inside it be?

"Ah, yessss," Dr. MacDeath hisses. He places the small birthday present on the palm of his hand. He bows at the waist and holds it out to you. "Take it!"

You jump back as the blood from his teeth splatters you in the face.

"Now open it!" he orders you loudly.

With trembling hands, you tear at the package.

Open it on PAGE 86.

You slam the door as hard as you can.

HONK!

"Uh-oh," Mickey cries. He flinches. "You slammed the door on the clown's nose!"

"Ignore the clown," Dr. MacDeath says. "Let's get down to business. The main activity for today is giving you a *scary* birthday! Right?"

You glance over at Sarah, the human swan. This birthday is pretty scary already, you think.

MacDeath opens his mouth wide in a grin. His teeth drip that red stuff all over your living room floor.

Gulp. What's this guy's deal, anyway? you wonder.

Go on to PAGE 99.

With your heart hammering, you leap out of the bushes.

Yes! MacDeath is only ten feet away — and his back is turned!

"Fire!" you shout, giving the signal to all your friends.

Instantly everyone lets him have it.

POW! BLAM!

He whirls around, and you shoot him right in the face.

KA-SPLAT!

"Aaaahhhh!" MacDeath cries. He sputters and coughs.

It's working! you think. He's choking on the stuff!

Pink, blue, yellow, and red paintballs explode onto MacDeath. You fire until all your paintballs are used up.

That's when MacDeath stops coughing. He glares at you with a stare of pure evil. Pure hatred.

Oh, no! you think, watching his weapon closely.

His arm twitches. He's about to fire that acid stuff in your face!

Look out on PAGE 64!

Alex is right. The pet store will take too long. You've got to get back to your house — fast! — and save Virginia!

But first, you have to win the scavenger hunt.

So you hurry to Alex's house, a few blocks away, hoping to find a dead mouse in his basement.

Alex grabs a flashlight from the kitchen. "The lightbulb down there blew out the other day," he explains.

Great, you think. Just what you want to be doing, checking out a mouse-infested basement — in the dark.

The two of you tiptoe down the cellar steps.

It's dark and smelly down there. His basement has a concrete floor that's always damp. There's a furnace, stacks and stacks of boxes, and lots of pipes running all over the ceiling.

"Where's the mousetrap?" you whisper.

"In the corner," Alex whispers back.

The flashlight he's holding is so dim, it barely lights the room. "The batteries are almost dead," Alex says as he shines it into the corner of the room.

The weak beam of light falls on an object.

"Yikes!" you scream.

Find out what's in the basement on PAGE 76.

You step outside with the doll and the noose in your hands. There's an apple tree in Sarah's yard, which is right next door to your house. You hurry there.

Quickly you climb the tree and throw the rope over a limb near the main trunk.

An owl hoots in the distance.

"No — not there," Alex calls from the ground. "Put the noose out near the end of the branch and hang her there."

"Why?" you snap at Alex. Climbing this tree is dangerous enough. Does he really want you to risk your neck, climbing out to the end of the limb?

"It will be more like a real hanging that way," Alex urges you. "We've got to convince MacDeath that this is a real noose. Go on."

Maybe Alex has a point. What should you do?

If you creep out to the end of the branch, turn to PAGE 11.

If you play it safe, turn to PAGE 73.

56

You decide to play paintball. All your friends love that game. You played last year for Alex's birthday.

And you're all totally good at it. You have a real chance of winning!

"Paintball," you announce to Dr. MacDeath.

"All right," he says in a deep, spooky voice. "Follow me."

What are you waiting for? Follow him to PAGE 72.

"Don't give up yet," you tell Alex.

You race back to your house and knock on the back door.

CLICK. The dead bolt unlocks, and MacDeath opens the door.

"What? You're done already?" he asks, sounding surprised.

"Uh, no," you admit. "We need more time. Give us a chance — please. We've got *one* good thing so far."

MacDeath narrows his bloodshot red eyes. He seems to be considering.

"Let me see — what have you got?" he asks, holding out his hand.

You open the Chinese food carton and show him your new purchase. "The mouse's tongue," you announce proudly.

MacDeath stares into the carton. Hard. Like he's trying to see something. Finally he lifts the little gray animal up and peers into its mouth.

"Ha!" he laughs, throwing back his head. More blood drips from his fanglike teeth. "This mouse doesn't even have a tongue!"

Turn to PAGE 95.

"We'll take the last three things on the list," you decide. "Bones from a graveyard, the murderer's knife, and pretty poison. You guys get the other stuff."

"Okay," Sarah agrees. "Meet you back here in less than an hour."

Sarah, Mickey, and Josh hurry down the driveway, toward Sarah's house. Then Alex turns to you with a worried expression on his face.

"The murderer's knife is easy," he announces. "We can use my uncle's fish-cleaning knife."

You nod. Sounds good to you.

"And for the pretty poison, we can get a piece of the bush in my backyard," he continues. "It's got pink flowers on it. But my mom says the leaves are poisonous."

"Great!" you reply. "That's two out of three."

"But what are we going to do for the bones from a graveyard?" Alex asks you.

You shiver and give Alex a solemn stare. What choice do you have? There's only one way to get bones from a graveyard. . . .

"But . . . you can't mean . . ." Alex stutters.

"Yes. We go to the Morston Cemetery," you say solemnly. "And dig some up."

Head for the cemetery on PAGE 113.

The blade on the hatchet gleams so brightly, you can almost *feel* the sharp edge.

The clown grips it tightly and raises it over his head.

"I've come to help," the clown says mysteriously.

Help? Great! you think.

Except for one thing. You can't tell if he's talking to you — or to Dr. MacDeath!

"No!" Virginia screams behind you. "Shut the door! Shut the door before he kills us!"

What should you do?

If you shut the door, turn to PAGE 52.
If you don't, turn to PAGE 74.

You decide not to open the door.

Dr. MacDeath's voice is so forceful you don't want to make him mad at you.

"Don't look so miserable!" he orders you. "You're supposed to be having fun! It's your birthday party! A scary-birthday-to-you party! Smile!"

He opens his own hideous mouth in a big, fake grin. His teeth drip that red stuff all over your living room floor.

Heh-heh. Start having "fun" on PAGE 99.

Dr. MacDeath shakes his head solemnly.

"That is a question we must *never* answer," he says quietly. "For your own good."

"But we *do* want to give you something," his dad offers. "A present. As a thank-you gift for all you've done for me."

"A present?" Alex asks suspiciously. "What is it?"

Barney walks to the front door and removes the spike that was locking you in. "It's waiting outside for you," he says, sounding like a television announcer. "It's . . . a new car!"

"A new car?" You can't believe your ears. Is he kidding?

"Force of habit," Barney explains. "I was a game show host before I lost my head. So now I give new cars to *everyone!*"

Cool! you think as you race outside to the curb.

Your friends all follow you excitedly. When they see the car, everyone goes nuts. It's one of those really cool electric cars for kids. Except bigger.

Big enough for all your friends to ride in it at once!

"Thanks!" you shout, jumping into the red electric car.

"Happy birthday!" Barney MacDurth calls as you drive off. "And be sure to always remember my advice!"

"What's that?" you call from the driver's seat.

"Stay away from streets marked DEAD END!"

THE END

Carefully you slide over to the tree's trunk and climb out of the tree. Whew! That was scary. But at least you're safe on the ground now.

"Let's get out of here," you tell Alex.

Then the two of you hurry back to your house. You walk up your driveway quietly, carrying the bag. Inside is the dead mouse, the turnip, and the noose. Three for three.

You might actually win this game.

"Where is everyone else?" you whisper to Alex. You thought Sarah, Josh, and Mickey would be back by now with their scavenger hunt things.

Alex is about to answer, when you feel a hand on your shoulder. You twist your head just a bit to see who it is.

Yikes! Your heart leaps into your throat.

Resting on your shoulder is the horrible, long, bony hand — of a skeleton!

Scream on PAGE 42.

"Aaaaahhhhh!" you hear yourself scream. "Nooooo! Please! Don't!"

You shiver at the sound of your voice. It's filled with pain. You glance at the cover of the CD again and read the title.

It says simply: YOUR FUTURE.

No! you think with a chill. It can't be. Can it?

Then you hear another voice you recognize — Sarah's!

"Don't leave me in here!" she cries on the CD. "No! Stop that! Owwwww!"

Sarah's eyes pop open wide. "Take that off!" she screams, covering her ears to block out the sound.

Dr. MacDeath simply walks over to the CD player — and turns it up. "Let's listen to the whole thing — several times," he says, laughing cruelly. "Unless . . ."

"Unless what?" you ask.

"Unless you'd like to open some more presents," he answers with a wicked smile.

Yeah, you think. Anything is better than listening to yourself being tortured!

Isn't it?

Find out on PAGE 69.

Your hands fly up to protect your face from the blast.

But peering between your fingers, you see MacDeath throw down his weapon.

"Look what you've done!" MacDeath cries, gesturing at his paint-splattered body. "You've ruined me! How am I supposed to scare anyone looking like this?"

Wow, you think, staring at him. He's right! He's covered in so many bright colors, he looks ridiculous.

He couldn't scare a three-year-old looking like that!

MacDeath's shoulders slump and he drags his feet as he slinks away.

"I'm ruined," he repeats, mumbling it over and over.

He walks off and disappears into the night.

"We did it!" Sarah cheers. "We got rid of him! Finally, we can all go home!"

"Home?" You stare at them. "But what about the rest of my party?"

Turn to PAGE 77.

"Nooooooo."

A moaning voice in the distance calls to you, warning you to stay away.

"Go-o-o-o-o-o."

"What was that?" Alex asks.

You shrug. "Probably just wind," you say, trying to convince yourself. "Let's get the bones and get out of here."

You hear leaves rustling. The sound of footsteps. Someone — or something — coming close.

You freeze.

"Did you hear that?" you whisper as softly as you can.

Alex nods. "Forget the bones. Let's get out of here."

"No. We need them," you say. "To win the scavenger hunt."

"Noooooooooo."

The moaning sound again. Closer this time.

Alex turns to run.

"Wait!" you blurt out. But before you can stop him, you feel something clawing at your back.

It feels like the sharp, pointy fingernails of Dr. MacDeath! Oh, no! He's followed you here!

You shriek as MacDeath knocks you to the ground.

Fall onto PAGE 109.

You're good at dodgeball. That's another one of the reasons you picked this game. You thought you could probably win.

Quickly, on instinct, you dodge the bomb.

Whoops! Big mistake.

The bomb rolls under the couch and gets stuck in the back corner, near the wall.

"You idiot!" Dr. MacDeath cries. His face turns even paler. "You were supposed to catch it — and throw it outside!"

A moment later . . .

KA-BOOM!

Well, you dodged the bomb, all right.

Too bad your chances of having a happy birthday just blew up in your face!

THE END

It's a tough choice. But you decide on the skeleton hand. You reach out and grab it.

"This one," you say. "The bones from a graveyard."

Dr. MacDeath takes the skeleton hand from you and sniffs it. Then his mouth twists into a mocking sneer.

"Ha!" he cries. "Those aren't from a graveyard! These bones have *never* been buried! I win! I win!"

Noooo! you think. MacDeath lifts the hammer and spike again.

He's going to nail the back door shut! Locking your parents out!

Hurry to PAGE 49 — and stop him, before he locks you in forever!

It takes a minute for your eyes to adjust to the dark.

Inside, the haunted house is a maze of rooms. Most of them are draped in cobwebs. A dim, eerie greenish light glows from somewhere down a long hall.

"Josh?" you call again.

No answer.

Oh, man, you think. Where did he go?

You take a few cautious steps forward and gulp.

You know where the green glow is coming from, you realize.

The floor. It's covered with something unreal. Something that looks like it came out of a GOOSEBUMPS book.

It's a green glob of shimmering, jiggling, goop . . .

Monster blood!

Oh, boy. You have a bad feeling about this.

A door stands half open at the end of the hall. Josh could be in there. But you have to cross over the monster blood to get there. There's also a huge ballroom to your right. It's very dark inside, but you can see fake, filmy white ghosts whirling around on the dance floor. But then you notice that one of the dancers looks more like a kid. A real kid.

Could it be Josh?

If you search for Josh in the long hallway, turn to PAGE 128.

If you enter the ballroom, turn to PAGE 26.

"I'll open some more presents!" you yell. "Just shut that off!"

You shout at Dr. MacDeath to be heard above the sounds of the horrible CD.

"I knew you'd see it my way," he mutters. He slurps a little to suck up the red stuff dripping from his teeth.

"So, my little birthday friend — what will it be? More presents from your friends? Or from *me*?"

If you open more presents from your friends, turn to PAGE 45.

If you open presents from Dr. MacDeath, turn to PAGE 75.

70

Congratulations — you won the game!

You came up with a noose that really was used to hang someone.

Unfortunately, the "someone" was you!

Oh, well. So you sort of *choked* when you had to choose a scavenger hunt item. Don't get all hung up about it. Just remember that if you want to escape Dr. MacDeath, you'd better not stick your neck out so far next time!

THE END

Dr. MacDeath pulls off his long, sharp, pointy fingernails.

"Oh, no," he whines again. "Why did you have to throw that thing through the *window*, kid? You got me in *big* trouble now!"

You don't know what to say. You and Alex just stare at him.

You know you're both thinking the same thing. How come MacDeath sounds so . . . so *ordinary* all of a sudden? And how come he looks like such a wimp?

You glance back outside, at the bomb.

It's just sitting there. In the pansies. It hasn't exploded.

Mrs. Jancovich walks to her flower bed and picks up the bomb. She turns it over in her hands. Then she marches up to your back door and rings the bell.

Open the door on PAGE 10.

Dr. MacDeath leads you to the back door.

There he opens his black cloth bag. He takes out six black plastic paintball weapons and six helmets with visors. He passes them out to you and your friends.

"Here's your ammunition," he explains, handing you a large backpack filled with different colored paintballs.

You put the backpack on.

Then Dr. MacDeath takes his own paintball gun out of the bag.

"Whoa!" Mickey cries when he sees it.

You gulp.

Dr. MacDeath's weapon! It's shiny and silver. It looks like — you gulp — like a real gun!

Dr. MacDeath sneers at you. He laces his long fingers through the trigger mechanism of the gun.

And aims it right at your head!

Duck on PAGE 130.

You glance down. No way! You are not going out on some shaky limb. You decide to hang the doll right where you are.

You slip the noose around the doll's neck and prepare to drop her from the branch.

CRRREEEAAK!

You freeze. What was that? The branch you're on shakes dangerously beneath you. "Alex — something's happening. You have to help me down. *Now.*"

But before he can answer, the limb begins to splinter under your weight.

CRAAACCCK!

"Helllpppp!" you scream. The whole world seems to fall out from under you. You hurtle toward the ground.

Whoops!

Looks like this is one time when, instead of playing it safe, you *should* have gone out on a limb!

THE END

"Shut the door!" Virginia screams again.

But you don't. You let the hatchet-wielding clown in.

He *said* he came to help . . . didn't he?

You swallow hard, hoping and praying that he wants to help *you*.

The clown glances down at you. "Get out of the way," he orders you in a no-nonsense tone of voice.

Then he turns to check over his shoulder.

"Come on!" he calls, motioning to someone behind him. "I'm in!"

Find out who's crashing your party on PAGE 93.

"I'll open one of your presents," you tell Dr. MacDeath. You stare at the three wrapped birthday gifts he set before you.

Which one should you open?

The little tiny one? It's the size of a box that would hold a pair of earrings.

Or the middle one? It's the size of a birthday cake box.

Or the large one? It's big enough to hold a television. . . .

If you open the smallest box, turn to PAGE 51.

If you open the medium-size box, turn to PAGE 78.

If you open the big box, turn to PAGE 107.

"Whoa!" Alex cries. "What's that?"

He stumbles backwards, and so do you.

There, in the corner of the basement, is the mouse. Caught in the mousetrap. Dead.

It's pretty gross — but that's not what scares you.

What scares you is the RAT! The *live* rat sitting next to it!

You panic and jump back with a small scream. You *hate* rats. They're fearless animals. Rats can come right up to you, bite you, and give you rabies!

"How did that thing get in here?" Alex cries. "We don't have RATS!"

You stare at the animal. There's something dripping from its pointed teeth. Which kind of reminds you of — MacDeath!

His evil laugh rings in your head. Could he have something to do with this? you wonder. Could he be using whatever magical powers he has to keep you from winning the scavenger hunt? You don't have time to figure it out.

Because the rat charges straight toward you!

Turn to PAGE 50.

"The rest of your party?" Virginia asks, her eyes open wide. "You mean you want us to stay — after all of this?"

"Yeah," you nod. "It's still my *birthday*."

Virginia glances at Sarah. Sarah shrugs.

"Hey, why not?" the girls both agree.

"We've still got all this cool paintball stuff," Sarah adds. "Let's have a paintball war!"

"Cool!" Josh yells, shooting a fist into the air. "A paintball war — with no one home! This is the best!"

Yeah, you think. It is.

And this may turn out to be the best birthday you've ever had!

THE END

Slowly, you lift the medium-size box — the one that's about the size of a bakery box — and pull it toward you.

Whoa, you think. It's heavy.

It lands in your lap with a thud.

"What's in there?" you ask Dr. MacDeath nervously. "It . . . it smells funny."

MacDeath doesn't answer. He simply smiles and smoothes his bald head with the palm of his hand.

"Open it," he says, speaking more softly than you expected.

Eww, you think. The longer it sits in your lap, the worse it smells.

In fact, it stinks!

Slowly, you tear at the blue-and-white wrapping paper. Inside, you find just what you thought — a bakery box.

Maybe it's another birthday cake. A rancid one.

"What is it?" Alex asks, moving in closer.

You shrug and run your fingernail under the edges of the lid, to loosen the tape.

Then you lift the lid.

Find out what's inside on PAGE 125.

"Here — catch!" you scream. You throw the bomb back to Dr. MacDeath.

He catches it without even thinking.

Instantly, his eyes open wide in horror.

"NO!" he cries. "Not to *me*, you fool!"

He opens his hands to drop the bomb. But it's too late.

The thing explodes.

You're expecting a huge *KA-BOOM*.

But . . .

Turn to PAGE 108.

There *is* a way to get blood from a turnip — and you think you know what it is. Cut into it with a murderer's knife.

"Alex — give me your uncle's fish knife, quick!" you say.

MacDeath gasps. And steps back.

Weird, you think. He seems afraid!

You kneel on the ground and hold the turnip tightly, so it won't roll away. Then you slice into the hard white vegetable with the blade of the murderer's knife.

To your surprise, thick red blood runs down the edge of the cut!

Dr. MacDeath backs away in horror.

"You idiots!" he cries. "You've ruined all my fun!"

"This is *my* birthday too, you see," he continues. "The one night of the year when I have the power to truly terrify kids! And now you've won the game — and spoiled it! I hate you! *Hate* you! I won't be able to do this again for a whole year!"

You gasp as you stare at MacDeath's face. It's starting to change!

Turn to PAGE 105.

Your heart pounds as you catch the bomb.
Now what? It could explode any second!
You juggle it in your hands.
Think fast again!

If you toss it out the window, turn to PAGE 14.
If you toss it back to Dr. MacDeath, turn to PAGE 79.

All at once you realize something.

It would be kind of *fun* to be Dr. MacDeath's assistant!

Hey — why not? You'd get to spend time wearing scary makeup. And dressing up in black clothes. And going to lots and lots of birthday parties. And MacDeath wouldn't be scaring *you* anymore.

So that's what you do. Except that slowly you begin to change things a bit.

Instead of the birthday cake full of live mice, bugs, and worms, you bring a dark chocolate cake. It has thick raspberry sauce in the middle so it looks like blood when you cut into it. But it tastes good and doesn't freak anybody out — too much.

Instead of twisting the party guests into balloon animals, you bring black balloons — and twist them into skeletons.

Instead of playing dodgeball with hand grenades, you play it with harmless black smoke bombs. It surprises everyone, but no one gets hurt.

Little by little, the birthday kids start to like you better than Dr. MacDeath — and eventually, you put him out of business!

That's right, you've become the life — er, *death* of the party!

Which makes this

THE HAPPIEST END OF ALL!

Dr. MacDeath unlocks the back door.

"Oh, one more thing," he warns before he lets you out. "You've only got an hour. If you're not done by then, you lose!"

"No fair!" Josh complains.

MacDeath reaches out and grabs Josh. "Maybe *you'd* like to stay here with me too!"

The long, sharp spikes on MacDeath's fingers scrape the skin on Josh's arm.

"Owww! Let me go!" Josh screams.

"Yes — go!" MacDeath shouts.

Then he slams the back door. And locks it.

"Wow," Alex cries. "You're locked out of your own house!"

Then, from inside, you hear a girl scream.

Virginia!

Turn to PAGE 120.

Dr. MacDeath throws his head back and laughs menacingly.

"The right answer?" he booms. "You want the right answer? Ha-ha-ha-ha! There *is* no right answer, you fools!"

"That's not fair!" Virginia repeats angrily.

MacDeath scowls and narrows his bloodshot eyes at her.

"Fine," he says to her. "I'll play fair. I'll let you start over and play another game. It'll be fun — since I just *love* watching you lose! Ha-ha-ha-ha!"

Then he points that long, sharp, metal-spiked fingernail at your face again.

"What will it be?" he asks you. "Do you want to do the scavenger hunt again? Or play something different?"

"We want to go home!" Virginia yells.

"No way," MacDeath says. He swipes his long, sharp nails at Virginia, just missing her cheek. "But I will give you another chance. You can start over on the scavenger hunt, or you can play paintball. Which is it?"

If you want to play paintball, turn to PAGE 56.
If you want to start over with the scavenger hunt, turn to PAGE 102.

You pick the first thing that pops into your mind.

"Party games," you answer in a trembling voice.

MacDeath smiles. "Good." He rubs his hands together. You glance down and cry out in surprise. Long, sharp spikes are shooting out of his fingernails!

"Ouch!" he cries. "I scratched myself!"

He puts his hand to his mouth and sucks the wound.

You and your friends stare in terror.

"All right — here's how it works," Dr. MacDeath says. "We play games ... until *you* win! If you succeed, if you win just one of my games, I'll leave. You'll never see me again. But until you win," he gives an evil chuckle, "I will stay — and fill your world with fear — even if that means staying *forever*!"

You gulp. An eternity with Dr. MacDeath? Nothing could be more horrible!

"Now," MacDeath says. "What game do you want to play? Pin the Tail on the Donkey? Paintball? Dodgeball? Or shall we have a scavenger hunt?"

You glance at Alex for help. But he just shrugs.

"It's your birthday," he says. "You choose."

If you play Pin the Tail on the Donkey, turn to PAGE 17.

If you choose paintball, turn to PAGE 56.

If you choose dodgeball, turn to PAGE 24.

If you want the scavenger hunt, turn to PAGE 96.

"Hey — cool!" you shout when you see what's inside the smallest box. "It's two tickets to Horror Place!"

Horror Place is an amusement park. You've always wanted to go there.

"Yes! Take me with you!" Josh demands.

Uh ...

"Okay," you agree. "Let's go."

Hey, you think. Horror Place is so cool! Maybe this birthday won't turn out to be so bad after all!

Hurry to Horror Place on PAGE 23.

You glance at the scavenger hunt items. None of them are quite right, you realize. You've got a whole mouse — not a mouse's tongue. You've got poison, but it's not pretty.

Then there's the skeleton's hand. You're pretty sure those bones were never buried in a grave-yard. They probably came from a science lab.

That leaves the noose. You went to a lot of trouble to hang Stephanie, the doll. You at least *tried* to make it into a noose and not just a dumb old rope.

You pick up the noose and hold it out to Dr. MacDeath.

"No, no, no!" MacDeath cries. "I don't even have to sniff that thing. I know it hasn't been used to hang someone — yet! But we can fix that!"

Uh-oh. From the glint in his eyes, it looks as if Dr. MacDeath wants to hang *you*!

No! you want to cry out at the top of your lungs.

But before you can run or scream, he grabs you!

Turn to PAGE 70.

Dr. MacDeath spins you around and around. Faster and faster.

"Hey!" you cry. "Stop! I'm getting dizzy!"

"That's the idea!" He cheers.

Finally he stops spinning you. He points you in some direction and tells you to go.

The blindfold is so tight you can feel it leaving marks on your forehead. You can't possibly use your old trick of tilting your head back so you can peek out from under the cloth.

Please, you silently pray. Please let me pin the tail on the right place. Then I'll win and Dr. MacDeath will leave us alone!

You stumble forward. Arms outstretched.

Finally you feel the cardboard cutout. You stick the tail on the animal.

"Ah-ha-ha-ha!" MacDeath cackles. "You *lose!*"

No! you think. Then you hear a sound. *GRRRR-RRRRR* . . .

What's that? A *growl*? Where is the sound coming from?

You don't have to wonder long. Under your hand, you feel the cardboard changing . . .

Into fur!

Pull off your blindfold on PAGE 98.

Suddenly the candles on your cake flare up. The whole room is filled with huge, blindingly bright flames.

It's so bright, you can't see anything but a hot white light.

Just for a second.

Then the candles sizzle and go out in a puff of smoke.

You blink. Your eyes hurt a little.

But when the smoke clears, you see something amazing.

Standing there in the room with you is the old bald man. The man whose head was in the bakery box.

Except that now his head is sitting on top of his body!

He looks normal — and alive!

"Thank you," he says, rushing up to clap you on the shoulders. "You did it! You saved my life!"

You don't know what to say. You're stunned silent.

"What's going on?" Alex cries.

"That's easy to explain," Dr. MacDeath says, smiling at you.

You glance at MacDeath and do a double take. His face suddenly looks normal too. No green make-up. No slash marks. No red rims around his eyes.

"This is my dad," Dr. MacDeath says, gesturing to the man whose head was in the bakery box.

Meet Dr. MacDeath's dad on PAGE 94.

"Is that really a murder weapon?" you whisper to Mickey.

He nods. "My dad used it to kill a rattlesnake when we were camping last year," he whispers back.

"Yes!" Josh shouts. "We did it! We won!"

"Not so fast!" Dr. MacDeath slams the knife down on the table. "First you must prove that the *rest* of these items meet my very high standards! And if they don't — you will lose! You'll all be my prisoners in a world of endless horror — forever!"

He picks up the red vegetable you brought and shoves it into your face.

"What, might I ask, is *this* supposed to be?" he demands.

It's a turnip, you think, shaking in fear. Isn't it?

Show MacDeath how you got blood from a turnip on PAGE 33.

Slowly, you tiptoe over to the corner. The mouse just lies there. Dead.

Alex finds a brown paper bag. Then he holds the bag open on the floor. You use your toe to push the mouse inside.

Whew. One item on the list down, two to go.

You and Alex creep up the basement stairs with the bag.

"What's next?" he asks you quietly.

"Now we need to get blood from a turnip," you say.

Alex shrugs. "I don't get it. How are we supposed to do that? Turnips don't bleed."

"Maybe MacDeath is trying to trick us," you mutter. "Maybe it's impossible to get blood from a turnip."

Alex nods. "That's what I was thinking. Let's go back to your house. We can see if Virginia is okay. And we can tell Dr. MacDeath that his game isn't fair," he says.

You're plenty worried about Virginia. But telling MacDeath that his game isn't fair? Hmmm. Does that sound like a good idea to you?

If you tell MacDeath his game isn't fair, turn to PAGE 46.

If you try to get blood from a turnip, turn to PAGE 117.

The monster blood sucks you onto your back.

"Help!" you cry.

The green glob oozes up around your shoulders. Your face. Toward your mouth.

Smothering you.

"Aaaaahhhhhhhhhhhh!"

You let out the scream of a lifetime. Pure terror fills your voice. Your throat.

ZZZZT!

You blink as all the lights in the house flip on. Blinding you.

When your eyes adjust, you see a dark form towering above you.

Turn to PAGE 31.

Your mouth falls open when you see two men racing up your front steps.

It's the police! Yes!

Dr. MacDeath lets out an angry groan. He begins to back away. "Spoilsport," he mutters, glaring at the clown.

The police push past you while the clown holds the door open. They grab MacDeath before he can run out your back door.

"Dr. MacDeath, you're under arrest," one of the officers declares, clamping handcuffs on the ghoulish man.

Most of your friends are speechless with shock. All except Alex.

"What's going on here?" he blurts out.

"I can answer that," the clown responds. He puts down the hatchet.

Read the answer on PAGE 48.

"Thank you," the man says again. "I'm Barney MacDurth — that's our real name. Not MacDeath. I'm sorry we had to spoil your birthday, but you were the only kid we could count on."

"Huh?" you say, not understanding. "Count on for what?"

"To help us," Dr. MacDeath explains. "See, my dad's head got separated from his body on his birthday, exactly twelve years ago. Since then, I've been trying to figure out how to help him. I discovered there was only one way to get him put back together — if somebody born on my dad's birthday would wish for it. On a birthday cake."

This is too unreal. "Why didn't you just tell someone what happened and ask them to wish for you?" you question MacDeath.

"I tried that last year. But the magic didn't work that way," he explains.

"So we planned this birthday party for you." Barney MacDurth picks up the story. "We chose *you* — of all the kids with this birthday — because we knew you liked horror. We figured you wouldn't freak out when you saw me in the bakery box."

"And you did it," MacDeath says, clapping you on the shoulders again. "You saved my dad's life!"

"But ... but ... but," you sputter, "how did your head get cut off from your body like that? And why didn't you die?"

Turn to PAGE 61.

MacDeath drops the little mouse back into the Chinese food container.

"No tongue?" you repeat, squinting at the mouse.

"No," MacDeath says with a laugh. "I know — because I bought that same mouse last week. When I got it home, I realized it was defective. No tongue. So I took it back to the store."

A defective mouse? Weird.

"Can we have more time?" you beg Dr. MacDeath. "Please?"

"No!" MacDeath booms. "Time's up. I win!"

He gives you an evil smile. "Now it's time to choose another game!"

Go back to PAGE 85 and choose another game.

"We want the scavenger hunt," you decide.

Inside, you're trembling. This birthday is a nightmare! But scavenger hunts are easy. All you have to do is go out and find everything on the list, then bring it all back to Dr. MacDeath.

If you do, you'll win. And he'll leave. You hope.

"Yes!" Dr. MacDeath cries. "I love a good scavenger hunt!" He reaches into his black bag and pulls out a sheet of paper.

You and your friends read the scavenger hunt list. There are six items on it:

1. A mouse's tongue
2. Blood from a turnip
3. A noose used to hang someone
4. Bones from a graveyard
5. A murderer's knife
6. Pretty poison

Eeew, you think. What kind of a list is that?

"Wow," Mickey exclaims. "If we're going to find all that stuff, you have to let us leave the house!"

Dr. MacDeath narrows his eyes at Mickey. "All right," he says in his booming voice. "You may leave the house — but only on one condition."

Find out what it is on PAGE 32.

You choke back a gagging feeling in your throat.

Your friends gather around and peer into the box.

"Okay," you manage to say to the head. "I'll help you. But how?"

"Find the rest of my body," the head begs you. "And put my head back on it."

Huh? How are you supposed to do that? you wonder.

"Do it!" Dr. MacDeath shouts. "Or I'll put *your* head in a bakery box too!"

You swallow hard.

"What should I do?" you ask meekly.

"Dig it up," the head says flatly. "It's buried next door — in Mrs. Jancovich's flower garden."

Whoa.

Are you really going to dig up a dead, headless body?

Or maybe there's some other way out of this mess. . . .

Like lighting the candles on your birthday cake — and making a wish.

You *do* believe in birthday wishes, don't you?

If you dig up the dead body, turn to PAGE 36.
If you try to get out of this mess by wishing on your birthday cake, turn to PAGE 133.

You yank the blindfold off. And scream.

Standing before you is a hideous, giant dog-creature — with six tails on it, all stuck in the wrong places!

It's alive! The cardboard beast has come alive!

It crouches down and lowers its head. Oh, no! It's going to attack!

Face the beast on PAGE 101.

"So what shall we do first?" MacDeath snarls at you. "Open presents? Play games? Eat cake?"

No one answers. Your friends are all frozen in fear.

You still can't decide if this guy's a clown — or a madman.

"I think I'll go home now," Virginia finally says in a meek voice. You can see she's trembling, but she marches toward the front door.

With only two steps, Dr. MacDeath reaches the front door ahead of her and blocks her way.

"No one leaves," he says. His voice sounds deeper and more evil than ever. "Understand? *No one!*"

"You can't keep us here!" Mickey challenges.

"Oh, no? Just watch me!"

MacDeath reaches into his pocket and pulls out a hammer and two long metal spikes. With one whack, he pounds the spikes into the door — nailing them to the door frame so you can't get out!

Then he reaches into his pocket and pulls out a key.

"And *this*, my little friends, is the key to the *back* door," he announces. "So don't even *try* to escape that way!"

You're trapped! Try to deal with it on PAGE 35.

"Uh, I'm going to open Alex's present," you decide.

"Good choice," Alex mutters under his breath, giving you an encouraging nod.

You grab the colorfully wrapped package that he tossed you when he arrived.

Then all your friends gather around to watch.

Your hands shake as you try to tear off the wrapping.

How come you have the feeling that there's something creepy inside? It's just a bunch of video games or something . . . right?

Finally you break the ribbon and pull off the birthday paper.

"CDs!" you exclaim. "Cool! Thanks, Alex!"

But then you see the shocked expression on Alex's face. He's staring at the CDs in your hands. You glance down at them and gasp.

There's a picture of *you* on the cover of one! You — chained up in some kind of torture chamber!

Find out what this is all about on PAGE 8.

The six-tailed dog leaps at you.

That's it, you think. I'm done for. This beast is going to eat me! You squeeze your eyes shut, waiting for the feel of its sharp fangs.

But nothing happens.

You open your eyes. The dog's tongue is hanging out of its mouth.

"Ruff!" It yips as if it's happy to see you. Wait a minute — maybe this dog wants to be friends.

"G-g-good doggie," you stammer. "Good boy."

"Ruff!" the dog barks again.

Hey, this is working! you think. Except for one thing. The friendly dog begins to wag its tails — all of them.

"Help! Run!" your friends scream, backing away.

But you can't run. The room is too small — and the dog is too big. One tail after another smacks you and everyone else in the head. Face. Arms and legs.

Each blow feels like you're being conked with a heavy board.

Unfortunately, you're being wagged to a pulp!

Oh, well. Looks like you were barking up the wrong tree when you chose *this* party game! Next time, pick a different one. But for now, you've got to admit that you've come to . . .

THE TAIL END.

Your heart pounds as you make your choice. You hope you're making the right decision. The one that will get Dr. MacDeath out of your house and out of your life — forever.

"We'll do the scavenger hunt again," you tell him in a shaky voice.

MacDeath crouches down and whispers in your ear. "Since I'm feeling generous, here's a hint," he says, sounding meaner than ever. "There is only one way to get blood from a turnip. Cut the turnip open with a murderer's knife. If you do, it will actually *bleeeeed*!"

You shiver at the tone in his voice. When he says the word *bleed*, he sounds like he's really enjoying it.

But is he telling you the truth? There's no way to be sure.

"Okay — let's go," Josh says. You can tell he's eager to get out of the house.

"Hold on," you say. "We're going to break into different teams this time."

Turn to PAGE 58.

You gaze upward. Dr. MacDeath is huge! Twice as big as he was before!

He towers above you, as tall as the streetlights. His body casts an enormous shadow that darkens your face.

"Hellllp!" you scream, terrified. You hope someone will hear you. Hear you and come out of his or her house to save you.

"Get him!" Sarah yells. She fires her paint gun at MacDeath.

Sarah's not a great shot, though. The paint hits him on the knee and splatters into the street. It pools around his feet.

In anger, Dr. MacDeath steps forward to grab Sarah. But he steps right into the puddle of slippery, slimy, pink paint.

"Whoa!" MacDeath cries, losing his balance as his huge feet slide out from under him.

Whoa is right! MacDeath slips on the paint and crashes to the ground on top of you — with enough force to squash you flat.

You *and* all your friends!

But don't worry. You can always start the book again, choose a different game next time, and keep reading until you find an ending that doesn't fall so flat! In other words . . .

A *GOOD* ENDING!

MacDeath rolls his eyes again. "You little creeps are going to be the MacDeath of me!" he jokes.

Ha-ha, you think. This guy's really funny — NOT.

MacDeath lifts Sarah up and untwists her arms and legs. Pretty soon she looks like a girl again. You sigh in relief. He did it! Maybe the guy isn't seriously freaky after all.

Then he opens the bakery box and takes out a big, fancy birthday cake with lots of roses. Your name is written on top.

"Now cut it!" MacDeath orders you in a booming voice.

You lift the knife and slice through the thick white icing. Then you start to lift the piece of cake onto a plate.

"Aaaahhhh!" you scream as you remove the first slice.

Bugs, worms, and mice slither out of the cake. They crawl and wriggle all over your dining room table!

Escape from the creepy crawlers on PAGE 119.

Slowly, the red rims around MacDeath's eyes disappear. Now his eyes just look tired. His teeth stop dripping blood, and their points vanish. His long, spiky fingernails fall off, leaving only short, stubby fingers with chewed nails.

Hunched over and normal-looking, he drags himself into your house to get his black bag.

"You kids are a rotten bunch," he mutters on his way down the driveway. "See if I ever come to one of your parties again!"

He walks off into the night.

"We did it! We won!" Josh and Mickey shout, slapping each other high fives.

You and Alex give each other high fives too. "Way to go," Alex says. "And, hey — now we can have a real party — with no one home! Let's order pizza!"

You nod. But before you can dial the number, the doorbell rings.

"Who's that?" Alex asks, opening the door.

Standing there is a guy dressed up in a magician's black coat and top hat. He has a strange look in his eyes.

"Good evening," he says in a spooky voice. "Where's the birthday kid? I'm here to create a *very special* party."

Uh-oh. Looks like this Scary Birthday isn't over yet!

THE END

"Okay — I'll stay," you decide. "I'll stay with Dr. MacDeath. You guys can go on the scavenger hunt."

"Cool!" Josh says, instantly heading for the door.

Oh, man, you think. Your friends beat it out of there as fast as they can.

They're *never* coming back! you realize.

Your breathing practically stops as you face the brutal truth: You're stuck with Dr. MacDeath.

Alone. Maybe forever.

You cringe as you notice more blood dripping from his teeth. You stare at the scars across his face.

He's so ugly. So totally scary. *Too* scary.

"Pretty good party, eh, kid?" he mumbles.

Is he kidding? you wonder. He thinks scaring you and your friends to death is *fun*?

He must be totally nuts, you decide. Wacko.

I've got to get out of the house, you think. Somehow.

Then all of a sudden you get an idea.

A brilliant idea.

Turn to PAGE 20.

You point to the big birthday present. The largest box.

"That one," you decide nervously. "I'll open that one."

"Oh, goody," Dr. MacDeath says, rubbing his hands together.

He pushes the large present toward you. His long, spiky fingernails scratch and tear the wrapping paper a little as he does.

"Sorry," he says with a chuckle. "But I thought you might need a little help getting started."

"Uh — thanks," you answer.

With a yank, you untie the ugly green ribbons. Then you tear off the shiny black wrapping paper.

"Open it! Now!" Dr. MacDeath commands you forcefully.

"I'm trying!" you answer. You pull on the lid of the brown cardboard box inside. But it's taped shut.

You struggle to tear the tape with your fingernails, but it won't come open. Finally you bite it with your teeth.

Your heart pounds, terrified about what might spring out at you as you lift the lid. . . .

Find out what's inside on PAGE 127.

The bomb in Dr. MacDeath's hand explodes — and shoots out a powerful spray of liquid. It covers his face. His clothes. His body.

"Ewww!" your friends instantly cry when they smell the stuff that's shooting out of the hand grenade.

"What *is* that?" Virginia screams, wrinkling up her nose and face.

"Skunk!" Mickey cries.

A stink bomb? Filled with skunk oil? Vicious!

Even Dr. MacDeath can't stand the smell! He runs toward the back door, unlocks it, and takes off down the street. Your friends sprint out right after him. Leaving you all alone — on your birthday!

Well, you're not stuck with MacDeath anymore. But talk about a *horrible* party! This is one birthday bash that really stinks!

THE END

"Ow!"

You hit the cold, wet earth with a thud.

For a moment, you lie there. Dazed. Confused.

Then you feel the scratchy claws on your back again. And a wet tongue on your face! Wait a minute — wet tongue?

In the moonlight, you see the silhouette — of a dog! A big, fuzzy golden retriever. He licks your face and nudges you with his slimy nose.

"Hey, get off of me!" you whisper.

"You okay?" Alex calls from the street.

"Come back," you call. "I think I found what we came for!"

Alex tiptoes back into the graveyard. Quickly you explain to him that the dog has wet, muddy paws — so you think he's been burying a bone somewhere. Probably nearby. If you can find it and dig it up, you'll have a bone from the grave-yard!

"No way," Alex says. "It's got to be human bones — from a real grave — or we won't win the scavenger hunt."

Really? Did MacDeath say *human* bones?

You can't remember. All you know is that Virginia is alone at your house with that creep. So you've got to hurry!

If you want to dig up the dog bone, turn to PAGE 131.

If you want to dig up a human grave, turn to PAGE 43.

110

A way to get blood from a turnip.

What is it?

If you've played this scavenger hunt before, you might know the answer.

Maybe you should tell Dr. MacDeath to bite into it. That way, that red stuff dripping from his fangs will get on the turnip — and make it *look* like there's blood inside.

Or maybe you should just cut into it with the murderer's knife and hope for the best.

You decide.

If you tell Dr. MacDeath to bite into the turnip, turn to PAGE 132.

If you cut into the turnip with the murderer's knife, turn to PAGE 80.

You edge closer to the dancing ghosts. The music plays on, louder. The ghosts dance faster. Some kind of strange waltz.

"Josh!" you cry. "What's going on?"

"Don't let the ghosts touch you!" Josh warns. "They're real! And their grips are like iron! They won't let you go!"

"Okay!" you agree, backing away gratefully. "But how did you get in here? What's going on? Why are you dancing?"

"She offered to teach me the waltz," Josh says sheepishly. "I thought it would be fun."

The waltz? *Fun?* Is he kidding?

Hey, you decide. Forget him! It's not worth risking your neck for some guy who wants to learn ballroom dancing!

You turn around and run out of there as fast as you can. Because ballroom dancing is just about the scariest thing that can happen to a person. And you've had a scary enough birthday already!

THE END

112

You can't believe your eyes. The object is round and black. There's a small computer on it. It looks like — some kind of bomb!

MacDeath presses a button. The bomb starts beeping.

"Dodge this!" he cries with a wicked laugh. Then he tosses the activated bomb right at you!

Hey! Think fast!

If you dodge it, turn to PAGE 66.
If you catch it, turn to PAGE 81.

"Oh, man," Alex whimpers as you approach the cemetery gates.

You look up and read the sign: MORSTON CEMETERY. Just the name is enough to make you shiver. Every kid in your town *knows* that Morston Cemetery is haunted. Even the caretaker won't set foot in the graveyard after sundown.

But Alex follows you there, dragging his feet as he walks. The cemetery itself is ringed with tall, thick pines. The trees have grown together so tightly that no one can see inside.

Only the entrance allows a slight view of the tombstones, lined up in tight rows. They cast long shadows in the moonlight.

"You first," Alex says, his voice squeaky.

You swallow hard and grip the shovel in your hand tightly.

Then you step through the arching briars into the cemetery.

Enter Morston Cemetery on PAGE 65.

MacDeath laughs so hard that his head shakes. With each movement, more blood drips from his long, pointy teeth.

"Well, well, well," he says. "Looks like I'm staying here . . . for the rest of your lives! Guess I'd better lock the back door — permanently! Your parents will *never* get in again! Your lives will be pure horror . . . for eternity!"

He pulls the hammer and another long spike from his bag.

"Wait!" you cry. "Give us another chance! Please!"

MacDeath whirls around and glares, thinking about it.

"All right," he finally says. "I'm in a jolly mood today. So I'll give you one last chance. But this time it's double or nothing. You pick one item from the table — just one. One thing from the scavenger hunt list that you think will meet my high standards. If the item is not *exactly* what I asked for, I'll make sure your world will be filled with twice as much horror as I originally planned. Now choose!"

You gulp. You feel your heart race.

There are only four things left on the table.

Well? What will it be?

If you choose the mouse, turn to PAGE 121.
If you choose the noose, turn to PAGE 87.
If you choose the poison, turn to PAGE 18.
If you choose the bones, turn to PAGE 67.

"What *is* it?" Alex asks again, squinting. "Is it a dog?"

"It doesn't matter!" MacDeath answers loudly. "Just try to pin the tail on it!"

Outside, the dark sky flashes with lightning. You jump when you hear a crack of thunder.

Did MacDeath somehow make that happen? you wonder.

Quickly, Dr. MacDeath grabs Alex, blindfolds him, and spins him around. He shoves a brown cardboard tail into Alex's hand.

"Go!" MacDeath orders.

Alex staggers forward with the tail.

Come on, Alex, you cheer silently. Beat Mac-Death so he'll leave us alone!

Alex jabs the tail forward.

See how Alex did on PAGE 134.

116

"Wait!" you plead. You turn to Sarah desperately. "Did you get the other stuff?"

She nods and hands two things to you. A noose that was used to hang someone in a high school play. A soft, velvety pink thing ... with cotton stuffing ...

"What's this?" you ask.

"Mouse's tongue," she says. "I cut it out of my stuffed animal."

"And did you get the turnip?" you ask.

Sarah hands you a hard, dry white vegetable.

"See?" you insist to Dr. MacDeath. "We got everything you wanted! We have the bones too. And the poison. And the murderer's knife. We win!"

"Not so fast!" Dr. MacDeath shouts. "Where's the *blood* from the turnip?"

You swallow hard.

Uh-oh. You didn't win — yet.

But *is* there a way to get blood from a turnip?

Figure it out on PAGE 110.

"Think, Alex," you coax him. "We've got to find it. We've got to get blood from a turnip. Somehow."

You follow Alex into his kitchen. He opens the fridge and reaches into the vegetable bin.

He pulls out a large burlap bag. Printed on the front is the word TURNIPS.

"Well, let's give it a shot," he suggests. He reaches into the bag and pulls out a large white-and-purple bulb-shaped thing.

"That's a turnip?" you ask. You've never seen one up close before.

"Guess so," Alex answers. He crosses to the counter and takes a butter knife from the utensil drawer.

"Here goes nothing!" He slams the knife into the vegetable.

Please, you think. Please let this work!

Find out if it did on PAGE 135.

118

"Run!" you yell to your friends.

Instantly, everyone darts in a different direction. You're all good at this. You've played paintball before, so you know how to take cover quickly.

When MacDeath runs off to chase you, you all give him the slip — and meet on the other side of the house, in a huge clump of bushes.

"Are you okay?" you ask Josh.

"My back burns," he answers softly. "But I think I'm all right. Thanks — you saved me."

"Don't worry about it," you mutter. Then you turn to Alex. "We've got to come up with a plan," you tell him.

"Right," Alex says. "And while we're thinking, pass out the paintballs. We've got to load up."

You nod and open the backpack MacDeath gave you. Inside are dozens of paintballs. Red ones. Blue. Yellow. Pink.

"I have an idea," Sarah says. "Let's all fire on him at once. We'll drown him in paint!"

Hmmm. Think that will work?

You hear footsteps outside your hiding place. Dr. MacDeath is closing in! Better decide what you want to do — fast.

Think about it on PAGE 47.

"Ewww!" Josh screams.

The cake is crawling with all kinds of disgusting creatures. A huge cockroach flings itself off the table, toward your feet. You jump away to avoid it.

Dr. MacDeath throws back his head and laughs. "Now, my little friends," he says, "what shall we do next? Play party games? Or open presents? Choose!"

If you play party games, turn to PAGE 85.
If you open presents, turn to PAGE 22.

120

A shiver runs up your spine. You and Alex exchange terrified glances.

You know you've got to hurry. You've only got an hour to find all the things in the list — to win the game and save Virginia.

You glance at the sky. By now, the sun has gone down. It's dark outside. A cat screeches somewhere nearby.

Quickly you divide up into two teams — you and Alex on one team and Josh, Mickey, and Sarah on the other. "Each team will find three things from the list," you tell everyone. "Then we'll meet back here in forty-five minutes."

"Hey, which three things should *we* look for?" Alex asks you.

Good question.

You stare at the list, trembling. The first three items are a mouse's tongue, blood from a turnip, and a noose.

The second three are bones from a graveyard, a murderer's knife, and pretty poison — whatever *that* means!

Both groups are totally gross. Which should you choose?

If you want to hunt for the first group, turn to PAGE 126.

If you search for the second group, turn to PAGE 58.

You decide to go with the mouse.

"This one," you say, pointing at the dead mouse in the trap.

"I asked for a mouse's *tongue*!" Dr. MacDeath bellows at you. "Not a whole mouse! That's like ordering a hamburger in a restaurant and getting a whole cow!"

You swallow hard and shiver in fear. Why is he talking about ordering food? Was he going to *eat* the mouse's tongue?

MacDeath pounds the table. "So you lose! And I stay here forever! Filling your lives with unspeakable terror!" he shouts.

He reaches out for you with his long, sharp, metal spike nails.

"Ha-ha-ha-ha-ha!" he screeches.

You freeze. Terrified. What's he going to do to you?

Turn to PAGE 123.

"Whoa! Look out!" Alex screams as the body begins to sit up in its grave.

Your heart pounds so hard, you're afraid you might faint — and fall into the grave on top of the body!

You leap backwards.

"No!" you cry as you watch the headless body place its two creepy gray hands on the ground. And lift itself out of the flower bed.

The neck — where the head was attached — is dripping blood.

"Stop!" you cry, backing away from the horrible creature.

But of course it can't hear you. It doesn't have any ears!

A moment later, the headless body runs down the street and disappears into the night.

"You let my body escape?" a voice from inside the house calls angrily. "Well, then — I'll just have to use yours!"

Whoops! Looks like your last chance to survive this story just got away! Oh, well. Better luck next time.

For now, you'll have to close the book and admit defeat. And don't you *dare* complain about this ending either! Because you ain't got no *body* to complain to!

THE END

No! you want to cry as Dr. MacDeath slowly moves toward you.

But you can't speak. Your voice is frozen with fear.

Virginia speaks up. "No fair," she shouts. Her meek voice suddenly sounds strong. "You can't do that! We won the game! That's a mouse's tongue right there! Hanging out of the mouse's mouth!"

"So what?" Dr. MacDeath shouts. "I told you — I don't want a whole mouse!"

"Fine," Virginia says, standing firm. "But if the mouse wasn't the right answer, what *was*? Which one of those things *would* you accept and let us win the game?"

Hmmm, you think. Good question!

Find the answer on PAGE 84.

124

Get Dr. MacDeath's weapon away from him? And then give him a dose of his own, horrible medicine? That sounds like the best plan you've heard in a long time!

You and Alex creep out of the bushes and call to him.

"MacDeath!" you shout. "There's something horrible in the bushes!"

"What is it?" he answers, sounding bored.

"A dead body!" you reply.

It works.

MacDeath quickly puts down his weapon so that he can crawl into the bushes to see. While he's in there, you secretly trade weapons with him. You leave him your own paintball gun filled with green paint.

"You kids were lying!" he bellows, bearing his bloody fangs. "There's no body in there! You're trying to trick me!"

"Yeah? Well consider yourself tricked, Mac-Death!" you shout.

You pull the trigger on his weapon — and shoot the burning acid at his face!

Turn to PAGE 34.

"Yuuughh!" Alex cries, gagging and leaping away from the box when he sees what's inside.

You gag too.

Because inside is a human head!

Head *over to PAGE 5*.

You decide on the first group. You tear the list in half.

"We'll take the mouse tongue, blood from a turnip, and the noose," you tell Mickey, Josh, and Sarah. "You guys take the rest."

Josh nods as you hand him the bottom half of the list.

"Okay," he tells Mickey and Sarah. "Looks like we're headed for the graveyard. Let's go for it!"

"Good luck," you call as they trot down your driveway. "And hurry!"

From inside the house, you hear another scream.

"Oh, man!" Alex moans. "We should call the police!"

"No!" you say quickly. "I think MacDeath really has some sort of supernatural powers. If he does, he'll zap us if we try to go to the police. We have to take care of this ourselves. We've just got to win this scavenger hunt. And hope he keeps his word."

Alex frowns. "Oh, great," he mumbles.

"It's the only chance we've got," you reply. "Now let's find a mouse and —"

"Whoa! You're really going to cut out a mouse's tongue? That's so sick!" Alex cries.

Turn to PAGE 30.

All your friends lean forward to see what's inside.

"Oh, man — it's just another box!" Mickey complains.

You peer at the contents of the carton and groan. He's right. There's another birthday package inside — wrapped up in red-and-orange paper with yellow crinkly ribbon all over it.

"I hate that," Sarah moans. "A package inside a package. It's so stupid!"

"Open it!" Dr. MacDeath screams at you fiercely.

Quickly you tear off the wrapping paper. Inside is another cardboard box. Taped shut. You struggle with the tape and finally get the lid open.

Oh, no! Another, smaller birthday present inside!

MacDeath cackles. He points to the third box. "Yes! I love this! Open that one now! Open it!"

You open box after box, only to find another, smaller box inside.

Talk about torture! All this box opening and no present — ever!

THE END

Nervously, you take a step toward the hall. You reluctantly stick the toe of your shoe into the green goop.

Your heart pounds wildly ... waiting. Waiting in terror for the monster blood to affect you in some horrible way. Just like it did in the GOOSE-BUMPS book.

Nothing happens.

"Yeeow!" All at once you feel a forceful, magnetic pull.

Pulling you down to the floor.

Oh, no! It's sucking you in! Sucking you in and swallowing you up!

You begin to slide into the green jelly-like mass.

"Aaaahhhhhhh!" you scream.

You squeeze your eyes shut tight and let out another piercing, bloodcurdling scream. "Aaaaaaahhhhhhhhhh!"

Keep screaming on PAGE 92.

From the slice Alex made, dark red juice seeps out of the vegetable, staining the counter.

"Well," you say. "It almost looks like it's bleeding."

"Yeah," Alex agrees. "This must be what MacDeath had in mind." He drops the turnip into the paper bag with the dead mouse. "One item left, but where do we get a noose?" he asks.

"We make one," you reply. "Just get some rope and make a noose out of it."

"No good," Alex reminds you. "It's supposed to be a noose that was used to *hang* someone. Remember?"

"So where are we going to find *that*?" you ask.

A strange glint creeps into Alex's eyes.

"I've got it," he replies in a low, sneaky voice. "Let's hang Stephanie with the noose!"

"What?" you shriek. You can't believe what your best friend is saying.

Turn to PAGE 27.

130

"Nooo!" you scream. You throw open the back door and run outside. You're not going to let MacDeath shoot you! Everyone else follows you, screaming.

Dr. MacDeath simply laughs. A deep, evil laugh. You glance behind and see MacDeath take aim. "Let the game begin!" he cries. His deep throaty voice echoes in the night.

MacDeath pulls the trigger.

"Owwww!" Josh screams, grabbing his back in pain.

Help Josh on PAGE 28.

Is Alex nuts? you wonder. Why risk digging up human graves if you don't have to? The dog bone seems like a better idea.

You grab your shovel and follow the golden retriever through the night. He wags his tail, leading you past crumbling tombstones. Finally you arrive at the spot where he was digging.

"See? I was right!" you whisper to Alex. Quickly you plunge your shovel into the ground. A few minutes later, you lift out a thick, half-chewed steak bone.

"Go. Go-o-o-o-o-o!" a ghostly voice moans in the distance.

"Good idea!" you whisper, swallowing hard.

You and Alex grab the bone and hurry across the grass. You run back to your house. There you find Sarah, Josh, and Mickey waiting for you in the driveway.

You glance at your watch. The hour is almost up.

"Did you get everything on the list?" you ask Sarah, panting to catch your breath.

Sarah shakes her head, looking scared. "Nobody can get blood from a turnip," she says miserably. "Nobody!"

Suddenly Dr. MacDeath bursts out the back door. A bolt of lightning flashes overhead. "I heard that!" he cries. "You failed to get blood from a turnip! I win!"

Turn to PAGE 116.

"Bite into it," you snap at Dr. MacDeath. You thrust the turnip at him. "Go on — you want to get blood from a turnip? Bite it!"

You try to sound really sure of yourself. Bluffing.

MacDeath grabs the vegetable out of your hand and tries to chomp down on it.

"Ow!" he exclaims angrily. He heaves the turnip into the night. "What are you trying to do? Make me break my teeth?" he shouts. "You lose!"

He gives you an evil stare. "Now follow me back inside. It's time to play another game!"

Gulp! Go back into the house and choose another game at the bottom of PAGE 85.

"I'm not digging up a dead body," you reply. "But I *will* help you."

Carefully you lift the bakery box with the head in it and set it on the table. Then you quickly stick some candles in your birthday cake nearby. You light them.

"It's my birthday," you announce · to your friends. "I want to blow out my candles and make a wish."

Alex shakes his head and looks at you like you've lost your mind. No one else moves.

Yeah — you know what he must be thinking. You've got a madman running your birthday party — and you're talking to a severed head in a bakery box! But you want to blow out your *candles*?

Still, something tells you this must be the only way out.

"Come on, Alex," you plead. "Sing!"

With trembling voices, your friends all sing "Happy Birthday." Then you blow out your candles. Hard.

I wish . . .

I wish the severed head would be put back together with his body. . . .

Find out if you got your wish on PAGE 89.

Alex sticks the tail to the side of the animal —
right smack in the middle. Nowhere near the end.
You groan.

Your other friends take their turns too. Blind-
folded, Sarah sticks a tail on the animal's leg.
Josh's tail ends up on the creature's face. Mickey
and Virginia both blindly jab their tails onto the
dog-animal's neck. No one has been able to win
and get rid of MacDeath.

"My turn," you announce boldly. Time to put
your plan into action. You glare into the bloodshot
eyes of Dr. MacDeath. "Come on — blindfold me."

"With pleasure." MacDeath gives an evil laugh.

He places the scarf over your eyes and begins
to tie it shut.

"Ow!" you cry. The silk cloth digs into your face.
He's tied it so tight, it presses on your eyeballs!

Turn to PAGE 88.

Alex removes the knife. You groan. The only thing dripping from the gash in the turnip is a tiny bit of clear liquid. It looks nothing like blood.

"Maybe we should try another one," Alex offers.

You peer into the bag — and see something interesting. You pick it up. It's about the size of a puny apple, but it's dark purple.

"What is that?" Alex asks.

"Must be some different kind of turnip," you guess. You hand it to Alex. "Try this one."

Alex holds his knife over the vegetable's dark skin. He slices into it.

You gulp. Will it work this time?

Turn to PAGE 129.

About R.L. Stine

R.L. Stine is the most popular author in America. He is the creator of the *Goosebumps*, *Give Yourself Goosebumps*, *Fear Street*, and *Ghosts of Fear Street* series, among other popular books. He has written over 250 scary novels for kids. Bob lives in New York City with his wife, Jane, teenage son, Matt, and dog, Nadine.

GIVE YOURSELF
Goosebumps®

...WITH 20 DIFFERENT SCARY ENDINGS IN EACH BOOK!

R.L. STINE

- ❏ BCD55323-2 #1 *Escape from the Carnival of Horrors*
- ❏ BCD56645-8 #2 *Tick Tock, You're Dead!*
- ❏ BCD56646-6 #3 *Trapped in Bat Wing Hall*
- ❏ BCD67318-1 #4 *The Deadly Experiments of Dr. Eeek*
- ❏ BCD67319-X #5 *Night in Werewolf Woods*
- ❏ BCD67320-3 #6 *Beware of the Purple Peanut Butter*
- ❏ BCD67321-1 #7 *Under the Magician's Spell*
- ❏ BCD84765-1 #8 *The Curse of the Creeping Coffin*
- ❏ BCD84766-X #9 *The Knight in Screaming Armor*
- ❏ BCD84767-8 #10 *Diary of a Mad Mummy*
- ❏ BCD84768-6 #11 *Deep in the Jungle of Doom*
- ❏ BCD84772-4 #12 *Welcome to the Wicked Wax Museum*
- ❏ BCD84773-2 #13 *Scream of the Evil Genie*
- ❏ BCD84774-0 #14 *The Creepy Creations of Professor Shock*
- ❏ BCD93477-5 #15 *Please Don't Feed the Vampire!*
- ❏ BCD84775-9 #16 *Secret Agent Grandma*
- ❏ BCD93483-X #17 *Little Comic Shop of Horrors*
- ❏ BCD93485-6 #18 *Attack of the Beastly Babysitter*
- ❏ BCD93489-9 #19 *Escape from Camp Run-for-Your-Life*
- ❏ BCD93492-9 #20 *Toy Terror: Batteries Included*
- ❏ BCD93500-3 #21 *The Twisted Tale of Tiki Island*
- ❏ BCD21062-9 #22 *Return to the Carnival of Horrors*
- ❏ BCD39774-5 #23 *Zapped in Space*
- ❏ BCD39775-3 #24 *Lost in Stinkeye Swamp*
- ❏ BCD39776-1 #25 *Shop Till You Drop...Dead!*

- ❏ BCD39997-7 #26 *Alone in Snakebite Canyon*
- ❏ BCD39998-5 #27 *Checkout Time at the Dead-end Hotel*
- ❏ BCD40034-7 #28 *Night of a Thousand Claws*
- ❏ BCD40289-7 #29 *Invaders from the Big Screen*
- ❏ BCD41974-9 #30 *You're Plant Food!*
- ❏ BCD46306-3 #31 *The Werewolf of Twisted Tree Lodge*
- ❏ BCD76785-2 #32 *It's Only a Nightmare!*
- ❏ BCD51665-5 #33 *It Came from the Internet*
- ❏ BCD51670-1 #34 *Elevator to Nowhere*
- ❏ BCD51673-6 #35 *Hocus-Pocus Horror*
- ❏ BCD51723-6 #36 *Ship of Ghouls*
- ❏ BCD51682-5 #37 *Escape from Horror House*
- ❏ BCD51706-6 #38 *Into the Twister of Terror*
- ❏ BCD39777-X Special #1: *Into the Jaws of Doom*
- ❏ BCD39999-3 Special #2: *Return to Terror Tower*
- ❏ BCD41920-X Special #3: *Trapped in the Circus of Fear*
- ❏ BCD43378-4 Special #4: *One Night in Payne House*
- ❏ BCD18734-1 Special #5: *The Curse of the Cave Creatures*
- ❏ BCD51674-4 Special #6: *Revenge of the Body Squeezers*

$3.99 EACH

- -

Scare me, thrill me, mail me GOOSEBUMPS now!

Available wherever you buy books, or use this order form.

Scholastic Inc., P.O. Box 7502, Jefferson City, MO 65102

Please send me the books I have checked above. I am enclosing $_____ (please add $2.00 to cover shipping and handling). Send check or money order—no cash or C.O.D.s please.

Name _____ Age _____

Address _____

City _____ State/Zip _____

Please allow four to six weeks for delivery. Offer good in the U.S. only. Sorry, mail orders are not available to residents of Canada. Prices subject to change.

GYG399

■ SCHOLASTIC

PARACHUTE

LOG ON FOR SCARES!

The latest books!

Really gross recipes!

Start your own Goosebumps reading club:

How to get Goosebumps stuff: clothes, CD-ROMS, video releases and more!

Author R.L. Stine's tips on writing!

Goosebumps on the Web!
http://www.scholastic.com/Goosebumps